"Just what are your plans, Mr. James Stuart?" Diana demanded.

"Besides marrying a woman you don't love and stealing my winery from me."

"My plans are my business, princess," he replied. "I've been at war with you for a long, long while. It's about time we had a decisive battle and declared a victor."

His eyes were fiery, and Diana felt a quiver of terror shake her body, and knew he felt it too. Just fractions of an inch away from her, he stopped, his eyes glaring into hers, his breath hot on her lips.

"Kiss me," he ordered harshly. "Kiss me like you used to when we were lovers, Diana."

Slowly she moved toward him and kissed him gently, almost lovingly. But his lips were hard and unyielding, wanting no part of her, humiliating her. He wanted no kiss; he wanted only tribute...

Dear Reader:

After more than one year of publication, SECOND CHANCE AT LOVE has a lot to celebrate. Not only has it become firmly established as a major line of paperback romances, but response from our readers also continues to be warm and enthusiastic. Your letters keep pouring in—and we love receiving them. We're getting to know you—your likes and dislikes—and want to assure you that your contribution does make a difference.

As we work hard to offer you better and better SECOND CHANCE AT LOVE romances, we're especially gratified to hear that you, the reader, are rating us higher and higher. After all, our success depends on *you*. We're pleased that you enjoy our books and that you appreciate the extra effort our writers and staff put into them. Thanks for spreading the good word about SECOND CHANCE AT LOVE and for giving us your loyal support. Please keep your suggestions and comments coming!

With warm wishes,

Ellen Edwards

Ellen Edwards
SECOND CHANCE AT LOVE
The Berkley/Jove Publishing Group
200 Madison Avenue
New York, NY 10016

Second Chance at Love

SWEETER THAN WINE
JENA HUNT

A SECOND CHANCE AT LOVE BOOK

SWEETER THAN WINE

Copyright © 1982 by Jena Hunt

Distributed by Berkley/Jove

All rights reserved. No part of this publication may be reproduced or transmitted in any form or by any means, electronic or mechanical, including photocopy, recording, or any information storage and retrieval system, without permission in writing from the publisher.

Requests for permission to make copies of any part of the work should be mailed to: Permissions, Second Chance at Love, The Berkley/Jove Publishing Group, 200 Madison Avenue, New York, NY 10016.

First edition published October 1982

First printing

"Second Chance at Love" and the butterfly emblem are trademarks belonging to Jove Publications, Inc.

Printed in the United States of America

Second Chance at Love books are published by
The Berkley/Jove Publishing Group
200 Madison Avenue, New York, NY 10016

CHAPTER
One

"IT WOULD BE a crime to let this opportunity slip away!"

Diana Kingston suppressed a smile as Gunther Werner raged behind her. Still, she hardly heard his words. It was his usual theme. She already knew it by heart.

Sunlight was streaming into the richly paneled study, spilling through the beveled panes of glass in the French windows where she stood looking out over her land, watching for the car she knew must come soon.

Outside, wide, carefully maintained lawns and gardens led down the hill to where row upon row of vines, hung heavy with dusty, purple cabernet grapes, lined the valley floor. The air was still soft with the warmth of summer, but there was a promise in its breezes, a teasing hint of autumn.

"If we don't do something fast, you might as well put a padlock on the door and stick a for sale sign on the gate," her companion went on harshly.

She pushed her thick, blue-black hair nervously back behind her ear and lifted her chin in the golden afternoon light. She could almost smell the tang of ripe fruit, almost taste the anticipation of the harvest, when the valley would fill with the scent of grapes as the pickers carried their loads to the trucks. The juice that came spurting from the crushed grapes could have been her own lifeblood, so wedded was she to the seasons that followed one another, the cycle of the wine-making year.

The cycle represented life to Diana. Her life. It was the only way she had ever known, and she loved every phase. But her favorite time was autumn. The harvest. The fulfillment of the grape.

The fulfillment of the grape was her own fulfillment, for Diana knew she would never marry. She had tried love once, and the pain of it still burned in her soul like the twist of an eternal knife. Unlike her lovely sister, Lisa, she could not flit from man to man, always hoping for something better. She had learned her lesson. Never again.

"The ruby cabernet was your father's dream. Are you going to let it die, as forgotten as he is, a casualty to the selfish, uncaring—"

"That will be enough, Gunther," she interrupted. He was ranting on more than usual. She turned to look at the slim, intense man in his early thirties whose pale eyes blinked behind thick-lensed glasses. He didn't mean to hurt her, she knew. His passion for the business of wine making prompted his outbursts, a passion she shared with him.

They both loved all of it—winter, the quiet time when the rows of pruned grape vines stood like an invasion of clumsy, gnarled gnomes, ready to pounce upon the unwary; spring, when tiny folds of furry green leaves sprang from the weathered branches like small gifts of life; summer, with its burgeoning joy as sprouts and newly minted canes raced to extend their bounty of green foliage and tiny, pea-sized grapes out to carpet the valley. Each period was a movement in the symphony of existence, repeating and swelling grandly as the years passed.

"I know that we must re-equip," she soothed Gunther. "I know we must modernize to achieve the quality we're after. It's my winery, after all." A sharp note had entered her voice at that last statement, which she regretted, but she plunged ahead. "It all takes money, Gunther. And money is the one thing we're short of."

Gunther ran both hands through his springy, fawn-colored hair, as though driven to distraction and on the verge of ripping huge tufts from his own head. "Money! Money is not my concern." The accent of his native Germany sounded pleasantly harsh to Diana as he spoke. "I am a wine maker. I am concerned with the quality of the grapes, the perfection of the wine. Money has nothing to do with it."

Diana sighed with exasperation. "Don't be silly, Gunther. When you haven't got it, money has everything to do with it."

"But the harvest!" He gestured wildly in the air. "Our cabernet grapes are perfection this year! If we could buy enough of what we need from the university experimental station to blend a ruby cabernet—"

"And," she broke in, "if we could afford to enlarge the aging cellars, re-equip the fermenting rooms, increase the cooperage—"

"But we could vintage date this year if only—"

"You know just as well as I do that we could easily get the money to do everything you want," she thrust in icily. "All we have to do is give up control to any one of the several corporations who have been sniffing around lately. Would you like me to do that?"

He swore softly under his breath. "Suicide," he muttered. "That would be suicide."

"Exactly." She had come to the end of her patience. "Please. I have enough to think about right now without this. Lisa is bringing someone to meet me." She glanced at the clock on the mantel. "They'll be here any minute." She stopped, her eyes meaningfully direct. Gunther took the hint, if rather gracelessly, and withdrew, muttering angrily as he went.

Poor Gunther, she thought with a touch of sad amusement. He was almost as bewitched by the old limestone winery with its mossy traditions as she was.

She turned back to the window and scanned the valley again, watching for evidence of the arrival she dreaded. Today she was to meet the man her sister planned to marry, the man who just might save them from having to sell their winery. He was also the man who might steal it all from her.

Steal was not really a fair word. Mr. James Stuart would not have put it that way. No, he would refer to it as protecting his wife's interests, for if he married Lisa, he would be acquiring a half-ownership in the winery. His financial resources were nearly unlimited, just what the winery needed so desperately. If Mr. Stuart backed them, they would be saved. The problem was, just where would that leave Diana?

At last, there it was. She heard the car in the driveway and immediately sat down behind the desk, bowing her head over a letter. Every word she had prepared to say had flown from her head. This was the critical time. The next few minutes might determine the course the rest of her life would take.

She heard the faint sound of voices in the entry hall, then a muffled laugh, and a pause that probably signaled a stolen kiss. It was a propitious incident, for it let Diana relax. She smiled to herself, enjoying a mental picture of a couple in love whose actions spoke more clearly than words.

Suddenly he was in the room. She could sense his presence even though there was no sound and she had not looked up. Inexplicably, a sharp, icy shudder tingled down her back, as though he had brought the first chill wind of the impending autumn in with him.

A tiny thread of panic rose in her throat, but she forced it back down. Keep working a moment more, she told herself. Let him wait. Let him be the first to break the stillness.

But apparently two could play that game. The stillness was not broken; it grew and grew until she wondered if she had been mistaken, and if he were really in the room.

Raising her head a bit, her attention still on her work, she widened her range of vision. Like a dark specter, he was there at the very edge.

Where was Lisa? The image of efficient control she was trying to project would work much better if Lisa brought him in and formally presented him to her, the head of the household. But Lisa seemed to be missing, and this silence was going on much too long. Diana would have to take care of this herself.

With a small inward sigh of exasperation, she rose from her seat at the desk, wishing her throat weren't so dry, her eyes still on the paper before her. She had to maintain an aura of businesslike control, she told herself sternly. Let him see she was capable of running her own winery.

Still looking down, she made a slight gesture that signified she was aware of the man's presence. "Mr. Stuart, isn't it?" she pronounced coolly, then turned her violet-blue eyes in his direction.

Her hand went to her throat. Shock paralyzed her, making her sway against the side of the desk. It wasn't

James Stuart at all. "You!" she gasped.

His sky blue eyes met hers with mocking amusement. Standing with his lean, muscular legs set wide in a challenging posture, he watched her reaction as though it were a sight he had waited a long time to see, and meant to enjoy thoroughly.

According to what she had heard, Mr. Stuart was in his early thirties, handsome and worldly, with a sophisticated, cosmopolitan background of wealth and good schools. He ran Stuart Enterprises with drive and imagination, but with a ruthlessness that made him many enemies. He had never married.

Today he had taken Lisa to lunch, and she had brought him by the family home so that Diana could finally get a look at him. But this man standing before her wasn't James Stuart. This was Jamie Morel, who she had hoped had vanished from her life. Yet here he stood in the very doorway she had vowed he would never darken again, under the very roof he had once scorned. She had never imagined this would happen. And now that it had she was unprepared for it, her emotions whirling in a sudden, bewildering turmoil within her.

For a long moment they stared at one another. He looked the same. So very much the same and yet so very different. The last time he had stood in that doorway he had worn dirty Levis and a plaid shirt that he let hang open to expose his suntanned skin to all her elegantly dressed guests. His thick sunbleached hair had been long, left wild and shaggy, hanging low down the back of his neck and waving untamed about his weather-toughened face. He had been shod in work boots, and his fingernails had been broken and stained with vineyard dirt.

This face looked much the same, still strong, with even features and an air of confident arrogance. It was a bit leaner, almost gaunt in fact, with planes that were harsher and more pronounced than they had been before.

But that was to be expected. His eyes were still a startling blue, his hair still a warm, sandy blond. But the rest was far different.

His hair was tamed now, parted low and swept across his forehead, trimmed well above the collar of his cream-colored silk shirt. He wore an exquisitely cut suit with the casual air of the well-dressed man. His shoes were of soft Italian leather, and his hands were manicured and no longer roughened by manual labor. His light tan suggested he'd spent weekends on a yacht rather than days in the fields, and his eyes were harder, colder.

"How did you get in here?" Diana began, but before she could go on, Lisa danced into the room like an errant ray of sunshine.

"Diana!" she cried. "So you two have met." Lisa turned a playful pout toward the tall man beside her. "I told you to wait for me in the hallway while I put my packages away. Now you've cheated me out of getting to see Diana's first impression of you."

"We've just barely spoken," he said in a low, resonant voice that Diana would have recognized anywhere. "There's still time to introduce us."

Diana looked at the two of them wildly. What was the matter with her sister? Couldn't she see that this man was an intruder? Where was James Stuart, who was supposed to be with her?

"Lisa..." she was finally able to grate out, but before she could say more, Lisa had launched into introductions.

"This is him, Diana," she said casually. "James Stuart. Isn't he wonderful?" The golden-haired woman was clutching at his arm, beaming up into his face, and the awful truth finally dawned on Diana.

"No," she said, her voice sounding as rough as sandpaper and feeling painful to her throat. "No, this is..."

But he was standing in front of her, holding out his hand in greeting. "What a pleasure it is to meet you at last, Diana," he was saying smoothly, his blue eyes holding her spellbound. "Lisa has told me so much about you that I feel as though we were already old, dear friends."

Without thinking, she followed automatic habits and took his hand in hers. His fingers were warm, strong, and he held her hand tightly—and much too long.

"Are you all right?" he asked, his eyes gleaming with amused concern. "You look a bit pale. Would you like me to help you?"

"No!" She pulled her hand from his grip and turned to stare at her sister, who was looking at her oddly. "Lisa," she began, "I have to talk to you."

"You do look pale, Diana," Lisa ventured. "Sit down. I'll run get the tea."

"Lisa, wait!"

But she was out of the room, and Diana was left alone with the imposter. The last time she had seen him they had not been alone. The room had been full of her friends, and that horrible girl had been with him.

Turning her gaze back on the man, whose tall, spare frame seemed to flood the room with electric vibrations, Diana glared at him accusingly. "She thinks you're James Stuart. When she realizes the truth—"

"Better leave it, Diana," he broke in, his blue gaze roaming over her face, his intimate smile infuriatingly confident. Suddenly his hand was on her arm, gripping her tightly as though to remind her of the physical superiority he could so easily assert over her. "Just play it the way you get the cards. Unless you want your sweet little sister and all the other people in your neighborhood to know about the real Diana, about that summer six years ago when you came to me in the night."

"Be quiet," she ordered with a quick, involuntary glance at the doorway that brought a chuckle to his throat.

"That's what I thought." His smile was mocking. "A pillar of the community now, aren't you? You wouldn't want your youthful escapades bantered about on everyone's lips, would you?"

The sun shining through the windows radiated around him, setting him off in a halo of golden shimmer that seemed to accentuate his power.

"You haven't changed much," he added quietly. "I knew you would be more beautiful than ever." His eyes suddenly softened. "Do you remember those days, Diana?" His gaze ran caressingly over her face, dwelling on her full red lips. When he caught her glance again, there was a curious vulnerability behind his hard eyes, a tentative searching that seemed to devour her defenses, and she felt herself sway toward him again.

He reached up to cup her chin, tilting her face toward him, and the room began to spin, the colors blurring in a wild, sensual melt heated by emotion. The only solid, real thing left was his vital essence. She stared at his face, going over each feature as she might the parts of a well-loved sculpture. It had been so long, but she knew each line, each plane, as though it had been only seconds before that her lips had clung to his in total surrender.

"Do you remember?" he whispered.

The memory was as clear as yesterday, but much more painful. She didn't want to remember. If she let herself go back to that time, she would find herself sliding into his arms, begging to be held and comforted, pleading to be reassured that what had happened that day six years ago was just a bad dream. That he had not taken her to the pinnacle and then betrayed her. But that would be a lie.

"No!" she ground out in a tortured voice, more as a shield against the power of his presence than in reply to his query, and at her answer the mask slammed into place again, turning his features to stone. He released her chin as though it had suddenly burned his hand.

"No, why should you remember?" he said in a voice

that was strangely hoarse. "There have probably been so many others since then."

He was the same as ever—arrogant, selfish, hard, and compellingly, overwhelmingly physical. But had he really been that way? It had seemed so at the end, when he had left her. And she had emphasized those qualities in her own mind as she'd worked hard to forget him.

But in the beginning he hadn't been that way. His easy laughter and brisk vitality had filled her summer with song. As those memories surged around her, she had to fight hard to keep from giving in. This wasn't going to be an easy battle, but it was one she had to win.

Gradually the room stopped spinning. Slowly she regained her stability. "What are you doing here?" she hissed. "Why are you pretending to be?..."

But Lisa was back with the tea that had been prepared before and held in readiness for this meeting, and he released his hold on her arm before Lisa looked up.

"I'm so glad we found you home, Diana," she chattered, flashing her sister a secret smile. "I've wanted you to meet James for so long." She set the silver tea service on a low table in another corner of the room and poured the tea into bone china cups. The dark man walked easily over to sit in a damask-covered armchair before Lisa, and Diana followed, moving jerkily, trying to organize her thoughts and decide how to handle the situation.

"You never come into the city, not even to visit me at my apartment, and James is so busy I didn't know if I'd ever get him to come up here to the valley to see the old place and meet my family." She smiled lovingly at him, and he returned her smile with a warmth that chilled Diana. "But when I suggested we drive here after our lunch in Sausalito, he said he could spare a few hours."

Lisa didn't know, Diana realized. She had no idea who this man really was. But then, how could she? She had been in Europe that summer. The summer of Diana's heartbreak.

But where had she ever gotten the idea that he was James Stuart, the wealthy industrialist? Someone had played a cruel trick on her, and now Diana must think of a way to extricate them both from the consequences.

A quick glance told Diana that her sister was immersed in playing hostess to the imposter. This handsome imposter she said she wanted to marry. Why now, of all times? Why, of all the many men who had wanted her, had Lisa finally chosen this one?

Lisa had always been a heartbreaker. From the time she had been a moppet with shiny yellow ringlets, she had been the object of general adoration. Diana could remember walking in San Francisco with her family and having perfect strangers stop to remark on how lovely Lisa was, not once thinking how their comments wounded the dark-haired girl they ignored. The male population of the entire neighborhood had been devastated by her beauty from girlhood on. Even little boys who thought girls were "yucky" sent Lisa valentines. And as she grew older the crowd vying for her attention only increased.

Of course Diana loved Lisa even more than the others did. But she couldn't help but feel some resentment, deep inside, as she was passed over time and time again in the general stampede to get close to Lisa. She blamed fate, not her sister, and felt for her a strange blend of pride and envy.

This early success hadn't helped Lisa gain a healthy perspective on men. In fact, it had cheapened their value in her eyes. Men were mere playthings to her. Easy come, easy go. For years she had flitted from one man to another as the spirit moved her, falling in and out of love as though the emotion were as easy to catch, and to lose, as a common cold.

It had been different for Diana. In all her twenty-six years only one relationship had moved her deeply. And she would never repeat that mistake.

She had stopped shaking. She was regaining control. Fight back, she told herself desperately. Don't let him destroy you again. She had to be strong.

Tossing back her raven-black hair, she held her chin high and stared into the man's face. "I understand you're practically a neighbor, Mr. Stuart," she said icily, sitting down on the edge of the richly upholstered loveseat next to her sister. "Some people say we may soon have to rename the valley after you. From what I've heard, Stuart Enterprises has been gobbling up wineries like animal crackers."

His blue eyes glistened with appreciation of her thrust.

"No, Diana," he responded, and she felt a shock at the way his voice lingered on her name. "Animal crackers are too cheap a commodity, and gobbling such a distasteful word. I've been lucky enough to gain control of two wineries in this area, it's true. But I think it would be better expressed as a rescue operation than as a gluttonous feast."

"I suppose that depends upon one's point of view," she answered acidly. "When a major corporation such as yours takes over control of a winery, it ceases to exist as anything resembling its former self."

"Oh come now, Diana."

There it was again. She couldn't stand the way he spoke her name. His voice sent gooseflesh crawling between her shoulder blades and memories flooding in from the darkest recesses of her soul.

"I think we've taken over in a very humane way," he said. "We've left the former owners in nominal control in both cases. They're allowed, within reason, to make all the decisions on the wine-making end. We've merely relieved them of the business problems, as well as provided them with an abundance of new capital to work with."

She could almost believe he really was James Stuart, the way he fit the part. Had she been crazy, thinking they could come to an agreement over control of the winery? The real James Stuart would say much the same thing, and suddenly Diana knew that her dreams had been naive. That sort of man would never let love come between himself and a good business deal.

"Relieved them!" she retorted. "You do deal in euphemisms, don't you? What you mean is, you make all the decisions and they get to stomp around on the grapes. Isn't that the truth of the matter?" She thought of the many old valley families who had suffered from corporate takeovers and especially of Millie Bradshaw, a close family friend.

"You take a hard view of it," he answered with a wide grin. For just a moment she caught a glimpse of the carefree youth she had known. Her heart lurched at the sight of that boyish smile, and she pressed her lips together, fighting emotions best left prisoner in her past.

"We've had a few offers ourselves," she blurted out, looking at him defiantly.

"So I've heard." His voice was low and expressionless, his eyes veiled.

"In fact, we've just turned down a very generous bid made by Kracket Industries." Diana gazed at him levelly, assessing his response.

"I know."

How could he know that? The bid had only been made three days before and had been quite confidential. As she had understood it, even the full board of directors at Kracket had not been filled in on the details. And Lisa had known nothing about it.

"So you can see, we aren't exactly a ripe plum waiting to fall into the right hands," she warned him, sensing danger.

"Certainly not." But his lazy smile showed how little he cared. She could see that he had other plans, special strings to pull.

"But tell me, Mr. Stuart," she went on with great effort, but unerringly probing for his vulnerable point. "Don't you want to get involved in the wine-making end of it yourself? Don't you feel a nostalgic desire to get your hands back into the warm vineyard dirt?"

The blue eyes had frosted over now, revealing the steel underneath. Fear trembled down her spine, for she could feel his anger. Perhaps she had gone too far. Well, he deserved it. How dare he come here and torment her like this? Just what was he trying to gain?

"No." He spoke with quiet menace, as palpable as a dark storm gathering on the horizon. "The vineyard holds no appeal for me at all."

Diana could sense Lisa staring at them both in bewilderment. Things weren't going as she had anticipated. Diana was throwing daggers that Lisa couldn't possibly understand.

"You must try some of these scones, James," Lisa said sweetly, leaning forward so as to block his direct view of her sister. "Diana makes them herself, and they're delicious. The jam is from our own grapes."

"Does Diana make that herself also?" he broke in sardonically, and Diana watched as Lisa smiled winningly to draw attention away from animosities and back to something pleasant.

For the moment she succeeded, and James began talking about the drive up from the city, the stop in Sausalito, the beauty of the countryside.

Diana sat quietly, a numbing mist enveloping her as she listened to the aimless chatter of the two people beside her. "The vineyard holds no appeal to me at all," he had said. But she remembered when it had been different.

CHAPTER
Two

ON A WARM, sunny day in late spring six years before she had just returned from an afternoon garden party. Lawrence Farlow had been there. He had recently graduated from Yale, and every girl in the valley had been after him. But he had chosen to sit with Diana. She had been full of pleased excitement, and anxious to tell her father all about it.

As usual her father had had little time to listen. Stubbornly she followed him about the house, trying to get his attention. When that failed, she had followed him down to the vineyards, still chattering away while he ignored her. He tromped up and down the dusty rows of grape vines and she trudged behind, still wearing the white organdy dress she had worn to the party, her hair still piled in a sophisticated twist on top of her head.

"Daddy," she said petulantly at one point, annoyed that he wasn't as excited by the conquest she had made as she felt he should be. "I want you to ask Lawrence and his parents over for a swimming party next Saturday. All right?"

"No." Her father finally turned on her angrily. "And stop your yammering, young lady, or I'll take you over my knee right here in the middle of the field."

He stormed off, leaving her behind, red-faced and furious.

"Oh!" she cried, hitting out at the nearest vine and breaking off a branch.

"Hey!" A voice cut into her like the sharp blade of a knife. "Watch the plant, kid, or I just may get in line to help administer that spanking your father was talking about."

Until then she had never paid the slightest attention to any of the men who worked in her father's fields. But now, as she looked up and met the insolent blue eyes of the man who had spoken to her, she felt stirrings of interest.

"Watch how you talk to me," she snapped back, becoming unusually rude in her confusion. "You may just find yourself out of a job. My daddy owns this place, you know." She knew just how snobbish she sounded, but she couldn't find another approach. Something about this handsome man disturbed her as no other man had ever done, leaving her cheeks stained with crimson, her eyes wide with wonder.

He stood before her with a swagger in his stance. "Your daddy may own all the land in the valley," he told her with careless arrogance, "but he doesn't own me."

His eyes didn't waver as she stared back at him, and finally, with a toss of her head, she ran to catch up with her father. But for the rest of the afternoon, as she walked behind him while he inspected all the vines, her eyes often strayed to the place where the blue-eyed worker was tying new canes to the support frame. Now and then her curious glance was met by his cool one.

Their path led them right past him as they returned to the road, and when she came within touching distance and felt his eyes still on her, a tremor of excited fear pricked the hair on her neck at the insolence in his glance.

His eyes glinted with amusement. "Real little lady of the manor, aren't you?" he hissed softly, for only her to hear.

Not knowing how to respond, but not wanting to pass by without saying something, she fell back on rudeness again. "Then what does that make you?" she said sharply. "A manor slave?" She was shocked to feel his hand close over her arm in a painful grip.

She looked wildly after her father, but he hadn't noticed a thing and was still walking away.

The young man was holding her so close that she could feel the heat of his body, and now she remembered looking down and marveling at how brown his hand appeared against her white dress. She gazed back up into his eyes and gasped as he tightened his hold and grated into her ear, "Be careful who you call names, princess. Before you know it, you might have yourself a slave's revolt."

Then she was free and running toward the road. But her arm burned where his rough hand had held her, and his blue eyes were emblazoned upon her imagination. Life was never to be the same again.

He had called himself Jamie Morel when he had worked in the fields that summer so long ago. And now he was back, no longer a worker but masquerading as an industrial entrepreneur. What made him think he could get away with claiming to be James Stuart? She looked at him intently, trying to read the thoughts behind his cool, guarded glance.

"Tell me, Mr. Stuart," she began, but Lisa cut in, her voice proclaiming her exasperation with her sister's strange behavior.

"Oh please, Diana, call him James."

"James," Diana mused aloud as she studied his reaction. "Somehow I would have said Jamie suited you better."

He had regained his humorous detachment, and his eyes glinted with amused intelligence as they met her cold, assessing stare. "Because of my boyish nature, no doubt," he answered with a smile. "Actually, I was called Jamie in my youth. But once I lost my childish innocence, once I abandoned my naive illusions, I felt that James suited me better."

Why did he seem to be wielding those phrases as weapons against her? Just what was he accusing her of?

"Are you sure you're not just using the dignity of the name to cloak reality?" She met his gaze steadily, though it took all her courage to do so. "A name in itself doesn't bring maturity with it."

"No," he agreed softly, and his eyes began a slow examination of Diana that left her feeling stripped and naked before him. "And maturity is a thing to be desired," he said in a tone so obviously sensual that Diana glanced quickly at her sister to see her reaction.

But Lisa had apparently given up trying to fathom this conversation. Not used to being ignored this way, she was staring down into her tea cup, waiting for the talk to wind down, a faint line of annoyance wrinkling her brow.

Diana had worn dark brown wool slacks and a beige blazer, clothes meant to instill in Mr. Stuart the impression that she was a strong, independent woman, someone used to taking command. But somehow the clothes seemed all wrong now. He was laughing at her, she was sure. The smile that had once marked a special communion between them was now slashing at her self-esteem, showing that her posturing meant nothing to him.

If at times she seemed to catch something else in his glance, something trembling on the verge of a questioning look, she was sure it was only a trick of the afternoon sunlight.

Abruptly she stood up and walked over to the French windows that led out into the garden. As she stared out over the late summer foliage, the murmur of voices behind her indicated that Lisa had regained James's attention. If they could keep up their conversation without her for a few minutes, maybe she would have time to conjure up some solution to this dilemma. Maybe she could think of a way to get rid of him.

They were in trouble, that she was sure of. How was she going to tell Lisa? How was she going to explain to her sister that the man she was in love with wasn't James Stuart at all?

But was he? She had been so consumed with her stunned surprise and her unwelcome memories that she hadn't really faced the possibility that he was really wealthy and powerful. She half turned and examined the elegant figure he made as he chatted over tea. She had to admit he looked the part. There was nothing young or untamed about him now. What she saw was a man in total control, a man of power and confidence.

Had Jamie Morel metamorphosed into James Stuart? With a sinking heart, she began to realize it must be true. And if James Stuart married her sister, Jamie Morel would be lost to her forever.

The sight of them together chilled her. He had pulled his chair closer to the loveseat, and his dark head was bent over Lisa's blond one, so close, so intimate, that it ripped a jagged tear in her composure.

Her breath caught in her throat again. Oh no, she cried deep within her secret soul. Please, please, don't let me love him still. I couldn't bear to go through that agony again.

James turned suddenly, his gaze meeting hers too quickly for her to mask the emotions shining there. For one long moment a tenuous bond shimmered between them. The color of his eyes deepened to a soft velvet blue, and she was reaching for him across the room, her lips parted in a silent plea.

He rose and started toward her, but Lisa was already up and pulling at his hand.

"I promised to show you our trophy case, didn't I," she bubbled, seemingly unaware of what she was interrupting. "Come on, it's in the den just next door. Diana will excuse us, won't you?"

Diana nodded wordlessly. The look she thought she had seen in his gaze was gone. His eyes were as flat and emotionless as tinted glass. She must have imagined it. What a fool she was to still harbor that tiny hope.

When they returned a short while later, she was ready, her vulnerability tightly concealed. "Have you shown Mr. Stuart the vineyards?" she asked a bit more abruptly than she had intended, swallowing hard as his eyes rose and seared hers once more. "You must stop and look them over on your way back down to the city." As James and Lisa sat down again, Diana remained standing, a clear hint that James had outstayed his welcome. But he merely leaned back in his chair with no sign of being hurried.

"Diana," Lisa trilled. "James has just agreed to come out and stay with us here next weekend. Isn't that wonderful?"

It wasn't the least bit wonderful. Diana had forgotten Lisa's plan to ask him.

"How thoughtful of you to arrange your busy schedule to allow us a few days of your precious time, Mr. Stuart," she said, a trace of sarcasm slipping out as she avoided his eyes. "You honor us."

"Not at all, Diana." His lazy blue glance seemed to reach out and touch her, sending new chills down her back. "A weekend here, with the two of you," he went on, smiling down at Lisa, "is something I've looked forward to for a long, long time."

She met his eyes again, and it seemed to her that they spoke much more candidly than his words did. He wanted to hurt her. He wanted some sort of malicious revenge on her and her family. The certainty of that brought a rosy glow of fury to her cheeks.

How dare he! If anyone deserved to get vengeance, it was she! After what he had done to her that hot, lazy summer so long ago, she was the one who should be searching for revenge. He was the one who had taken her young, innocent heart and flung it to the winds. He was the one who had shown her what love could be, helping her construct a golden castle from dreams snatched out of the summer breezes. And he was the one who had smashed that castle before her eyes, crushing every shining rampart, until it lay before her in the dust that soaked up her tears.

Those memories still stung. She pushed them away and turned back to the man who had stirred them from their slumber.

"We do have your address in the city, don't we, Mr. Stuart? In case we need to get in touch with you for some reason?"

He was assessing her intently, analyzing her words and probably wondering what her angle was. "Everyone knows where to find the Stuart Building, Diana. My offices are well known."

"No." She smiled nervously, wondering why she felt

she must make such a point of it. "I meant your home address. You do have a home address?"

"Of course. Your sister has been to my apartment and must have the address."

A sudden hot flash of pain slashed through Diana's chest at the thought of Lisa in this man's home. She glanced at her sister, but saw only the warm glow of friendly affection in her eyes. There had been nothing serious between them. Not yet. But what would happen if Diana didn't do something to stop it? Her hands were icy and she rubbed them together before her, twisting her fingers in a tortured knot.

Just how far had it gone? Was Lisa really in love? She had said this man attracted her as few others ever had. What if? . . . But that did not bear thinking of, and Diana returned to her original goal.

"Let me have the address, please," she said crisply, pulling a slip of paper from the desk. "And your telephone number. Just in case we have to cancel for any reason."

She smiled sweetly at James and was unsettled to find him chuckling. "Of course," he said, not bothering to conceal his amusement. He gave her the information she sought, then rose.

"Lisa, I really must get back. I want to clear up all the loose ends so that I'll have a full weekend, uninterrupted by business, to devote to you."

"Of course, James." Lisa rose gracefully and Diana had to grit her teeth to keep from protesting her sister's willingness to do as this arrogant man bid.

"It was a rare pleasure meeting you this way, Diana." He was so tall, well over six feet, that Diana felt an involuntary surge of emotion at his nearness. She had to tilt her head back to look into his eyes, and then his hand closed over hers, and his warmth seemed to flow about her as it had that day in the vineyard, taking her breath away, extending the moment into an eternity as she lost her way among the cloudy blue mists of his gaze.

Then he and Lisa were gone, out the door and down the driveway, and an overwhelming sadness numbed her, a sense of loss that she was unable to explain.

It was only her unease, she told herself. Jamie had reappeared in her life for a reason, she was sure of it. And if he married Lisa, he would take control of the winery.

Her gaze settled on the land again, the rich, warm earth, the burgeoning grape vines. A fierce determination swept over her. She wasn't going to lose her winery. She would fight to keep it with all her strength.

The winery had filled her life since the summer when she had known Jamie Morel. She had gone away to college that fall. School had been fun, but it had seemed to her a waiting period, a marking of time until she could get back to her real aim in life—running the winery.

Her parents had both died shortly after her college graduation, and the state of affairs she had been left with had not been ideal. It had taken most of the last two years to straighten things out.

They were selling more wine than ever now. But they had reached a point where they must modernize and expand their operation or begin rapidly to lose all the ground they had gained so far. Diana had been over the figures with the accountant again and again. A tremendous infusion of capital was mandatory.

Many of the other wineries in the area were facing exactly this problem. And most of them were selling out to major corporations, gaining a handy profit but saying goodbye to the life they loved. Diana had hoped to avoid that move.

But now there was a new threat. Could she avoid James Stuart's power? He had a power over her the others didn't have.

* * *

Diana stopped her ancient Triumph with its chipped green racing stripe at the edge of the vineyards. She turned off the engine and sat staring into the field. Rows of vines stood in the early evening twilight like a stalwart honor guard, all in full, bright green leaf and still holding their wealth of purple gold in their gnarled arms.

This was where it had happened. This was where she had first seen Jamie Morel.

For days after that first meeting she had driven this very car, newly acquired as a high school graduation present from her father, up and down this valley road, going into town on any pretext whatsoever. Anything just to get another glimpse of the blue-eyed fieldworker who had set her pulse aflame as no man had ever done before.

Usually he was nowhere in sight, but occasionally he would be working close enough to the road to give her one more mental picture to carry with her to bed at night. A few times she was even able to catch his eye, and though he didn't smile, he watched her, standing up to follow the progress of her car all the way up the hill. How her heart would thump when she caught sight of him in her rear-view mirror!

She smiled now, remembering. It had been good then. She had been in the throes of her first serious crush. The first and only one she'd ever had.

The hours she had spent plotting how to get close enough to talk to him again! Finally she had used the classic ploy—car trouble.

He had come to her aid readily enough, though he wasn't able to find the ominous clank she was sure she had heard in the engine. It had been a hot day, and he wasn't wearing a shirt. As he bent to take a look under the hood, she studied his glistening flesh, so firm and slick in the summer sunlight. A numbing warmth flooded through her, leaving her somewhat dazed. As he stood and turned to face her, an overwhelming compulsion guided her hand to his chest, and she lightly touched the damp, brown skin as she stared into his eyes, her lips slightly parted, her eyes misted by a strange dullness. She had stood there, so young and vulnerable, her black hair pulled back at the sides of her head in two long pony tails, her slim body displayed in tight jeans and a bright pink tube top. She had known his power over her.

She remembered so clearly his half grin as he pushed her hand away. "If that's what you want," he had said softly, "you had better come see me at night." With a jerk of his head, he had indicated the rise of land known as Lion Mesa, because, in the century past, it had harbored a mountain lion's den. "I keep my bed roll up there. You're welcome any time, princess."

The grin had ripened into a chuckle as he turned away from her and walked casually back to his work, and back to the jokes and whistles of his fellow workers.

As she thought of it now, her hands clenched into fists, her fingernails biting into her flesh. She hated him, hated him with all the rage that was in her, just as she had once loved him with all the passion.

That passion, be it hatred or love, had crippled her to some degree. It had been a long time after his betrayal before she could even think of dating another man. In the spring of her freshman year at college she had finally taken the step by agreeing to attend a picnic with a fellow botany major. Noticing that she was dating again, other potential beaux began to appear regularly. But even after she had returned to a normal social life, she had been unable to break the pattern of reserve and distrust. There had never been another love in her life. The dating she did was strictly casual. If ever a man showed any sign of wanting something more, she turned her back with not a second glance.

Lately dating hadn't seemed worth the effort, and she had wrapped herself up in work, not even joining old friends at the tennis club or attending the parties of her contemporaries. It was a lonely life, but a relatively painless one.

Abruptly she turned the key in its switch and coaxed the engine back into a roar. Her purpose was reaffirmed. She had to do something about Jamie Morel or James Stuart or whoever he was, and she had to do it soon.

The first step would be a visit with Millie Bradshaw, who had let it be known that she thought Lisa and James a perfect match. She moved in the top social circles of the city and had, in fact, been the one to introduce the two of them. If anyone knew anything about what James Stuart might be up to, it would be Millie.

As Diana turned from the highway onto the road that led to Goldcrest Winery, she noted with distaste the newly paved surface of the widened entryway. Ever since she could remember, the entry had been lined with ancient, crumbling cobblestones that had been laid in the middle of the last century. But two years earlier Goldcrest Winery had been taken over by a large corporation, Koler Foods, and now the modernization had begun.

Diana did not aim her little car for the new, gleaming steel and glass building at the top of the hill, but turned instead down a tiny lane that led to a small frame cottage set cozily among black oaks. Country roses twined about the doorway, and a fat red tabby cat rubbed its silky fur against her legs as she stepped onto the rickety porch.

The sun had sunk below the horizon, and the shadows were deepening to a purple haze as Diana reached the door, but no light burned inside. The first feeling that hit her was one of disappointment. Millie must be away. Then she noticed a movement within and realized her friend was sitting in a rocker near the far window, gazing out at the darkening landscape and rocking the evening away.

"Millie!" she called, rather than knocking, and saw the chair stop before a spry, slim, animated woman in her later years came hurrying to the door to let Diana in.

"Diana! I don't know what got into me. I lost track of the time." She switched on a light as she let the younger woman into her house, bustling about the room in a way that told Diana she had been embarrassed to be caught sitting in the darkness, dreaming.

Something about her mood touched Diana and drew her attention all the more to what Millie had been doing. Other incidental details that she had noticed in the last few months loomed larger than they had as individual incidents. Something was bothering Millie, Diana was sure of it. Suddenly her friend's peace of mind seemed much more important than coming to terms with James Stuart.

She sat down opposite Millie on the overstuffed rattan chair in the tiny living room and gazed with concern into the tired, slightly watery, pale blue eyes.

"Millie," she said softly, "what is it?"

The little woman smiled her wide, carefree smile just as she always did, but Diana could see that there had been an erosion in her well-being. She silently chastised herself for not having noticed sooner.

"Oh, Diana, there's nothing the matter with me. I'm just fine. And I'm just dying to hear all about your interview with James Stuart. Tell me!"

Diana shook her head slowly. "I will, Millie. But first I want to know about you." She noticed a resistance in her friend's expression and leaned forward suddenly, grasping both of Millie's hands in her own. "Something is bothering you, I know it." She squeezed the thin, blue-veined hands warmly. "Millie, we've been friends for too long for you to try to fool me. Part of friendship is giving of yourself." She smiled into the pale eyes. "So come on and give! I want to know what this is all about."

Millie pulled her hands from Diana's grasp and rose slowly to her feet. Diana could see the emotions warring behind the kindly eyes—doubt, embarrassment, hesitancy, and finally an eagerness to unburden herself. At last the latter won out.

She turned to stare out the large bay window, out over the fields of golden grass and hay. With her back to her friend, she spoke rapidly.

"All right, Diana, I'll tell you. I was just going through a melancholy moment. Sometimes... sometimes I just feel as though the world were a great big hay wagon with everyone hanging on for dear life, and somehow I fell off when we rounded a tight curve. The rest of you are headed for the future, but I won't ever catch up again."

"Oh, Millie!" Diana rose and threw an arm around the tiny woman's shoulders. "How can you say such a thing? You've got more life in you than any teenager I know."

She knew the words were empty, that they really meant nothing more than the hug did, but she couldn't think of any other way to tell Millie how much she was loved, what a difference she made in the lives of other people. Useless words, but Millie rewarded them with a big smile behind which Diana could search out no lingering depression.

"Of course you're right," Millie agreed with all her old sparkle. "And it's trying to keep up with you and your sister that keeps me so young. Now tell me, what happened with the corporation king?"

They sat down again, and Diana took a moment to

rethink her intentions. She didn't want to worry Millie with her own problems at a time like this. Better to tell her the surface of what had happened and see what there was to be gleaned from her reactions.

"Lisa brought him by, just as we planned," she began.

"Well?" Millie crowed. "Wasn't he just as marvelous as I said he would be? I tell you, the moment I saw him, I knew he was perfect for your sister."

Diana flashed her a questioning look. "I don't think you ever did tell me just where you met him, Millie. Have you known him for long?"

Millie shook her head. "No, not long. In fact, I think he was overseas for several years, building up his fortune, as it were. The Stuart Building itself was built years ago, when his father ran the business."

"Did you know his father?"

"No. That is, only by sight and reputation. He wasn't one to socialize. There was some mysterious tragedy in his past, but I don't think I ever knew exactly what it was. Something about his wife leaving him."

Diana sighed. "But you do like James Stuart, don't you? Cold and calculating though he is?"

Millie looked amazed. "Cold and calculating? Why, I never heard of such a thing! He's one of the dearest men. He certainly always has a nice smile for me."

Diana frowned, wondering if they were talking about the same person. But the longer she spoke to her friend, the more she was convinced that James Stuart was a favorite of Millie's and that she hoped the match with Lisa would come off.

Millie had been especially interested in doing anything she could to help keep Diana's winery from falling to outside control, as Millie's had. The Bradshaw family had run Goldcrest Winery for generations, just as the Kingstons had run their own. Since their land adjoined, the two families had always been close. Millie was more like an aging aunt than a neighbor to Diana. And when Millie's husband, Herbert, had died, and Millie had been forced to sell out the winery and the vineyards, keeping for herself only the tiny cottage that had once housed the vineyard overseer, Diana had seen the writing on the wall.

Koler Foods had paid a tidy sum for the place, but much of it had gone to cover debts that had accrued over the years as the Bradshaws tried to make the winery pay during times of bad grapes and faulty equipment. She had enough to live on quite comfortably, and she kept up her membership in her city organizations and in the tennis and country clubs. But there wasn't much more than that. And there didn't seem to be much left to make life worthwhile. All Millie had ever done was run the winery. But Koler Foods had people they felt were more qualified to do the job, and Millie had been left to stare out bay windows at the setting sun.

The situation at Kingston Winery was somewhat better than Millie's had been. Diana had few outstanding debts, and the grape harvests had been getting better every year. But the cooperage was old and needed to be replaced. Some fields needed replanting and others updating. The modest success the Kingston label had enjoyed was just that—modest. In order to begin to show a nice profit, they had to renovate and expand. All that took money, which Diana didn't have.

Already representatives of several large concerns had been by to point out these problems to Diana, to announce casually that their firms might be willing to consider "bailing her out." In exchange for control of the winery, of course. Diana's blood ran cold at the thought of being cast aside, useless, superfluous, a has-been in the industry she loved. She couldn't let it happen. She had been desperate to find a way to avoid it. And Millie was behind her all the way. When Millie had suggested that

Sweeter Than Wine

James Stuart would have the resources to back the winery, she had thought it would be the answer to all their prayers. For a short time Diana had thought she might be right. Now she knew better.

As Diana was preparing to leave, she looked out into the darkness and remembered the sad thoughts Millie had admitted to earlier in their visit.

"Listen," she said impulsively. "I want you to promise me something. I'm going to give you my friend Beth Wheeler's card." She pulled out her purse and dug in it for the item. "I want you to call her about that volunteer work."

Reluctance clouded Millie's face. "Oh I don't know, Diana," she said slowly. "We've talked about this before. I'm too old-fashioned to be of any use."

"Don't talk that way," Diana scolded. "Before you know it, you'll begin to believe it." She hugged her friend, then placed the social worker's card firmly in Millie's hand. "Beth always has some project going. It'll do you good to be involved in something again."

As she drove away, she wondered if soon she would have to take her own advice. But if it came to that, she would be looking for a whole new career.

CHAPTER
Three

IT TOOK ONLY a little over an hour to drive into San Francisco in the morning, and no time at all to find the Stuart Building. Centrally located near Union Square and Chinatown, it was all tinted glass and strong, straight lines, with plush carpeting in the hallways and music in the elevators.

Mr. Stuart's secretary was an efficient-looking, matronly woman who appeared doubtful when she heard Diana's name.

"He's tied up today," she warned her. "And without an appointment, I can't promise—"

"This is very urgent," Diana insisted. "And quite personal. Please let Mr. Stuart know that I'm here. If you tell him I run Kingston Winery, that might smooth things."

"Ah, a winery," the woman said, her eyes lighting up at the mention of it. Obviously the rumors that James was fascinated with the idea of becoming a major vintner were not exaggerated.

But before the woman could let her employer know about his caller, a group of senior citizens swept into the office, their tempers high and voices raised, and Diana watched with growing impatience as the woman tried to tend to their loud list of complaints.

"He's taking the roof right from over our heads," was the sentence that rang out most clearly. "Where are we going to go if he takes our homes from us?"

In other circumstances Diana might have had some sympathy for their pleas, but right now her mind was filled with her own problems.

She could see the door that must lead to James's office. All she really had to do was walk quickly down the little hall, open the door, and she would have achieved her goal. If she had to wait until the problems of this vocal group were straightened out, she might be here all day.

She glanced at the secretary and saw that she was totally engulfed in the arguments around her. No one was paying any attention to her. After a quick, cursory glance around the area, Diana clutched her purse in her hand and strode quickly down the hall to the solid oak door.

She saw no point in knocking. That would only give him another chance to keep her out. Drawing a deep breath, she squared her shoulders and flung open the door.

The room was richly furnished with polished wood and antique accoutrements that surprised her in so con-

Sweeter Than Wine   37

temporary a building. The huge desk was efficiently modern, but sported legs of oak carved in the elaborate style of the Louis XV period, and the bookcases that lined the side walls echoed that style. The wall behind the desk was made of solid glass and looked out over the city in an awesome view.

The office was empty. Diana closed the door behind her and walked over to the desk, hoping to see a framed picture or some other object that would help her get a fix on this man she had come to consult. But there were no photographs. The desk was strewn with papers, but the only personal item was a sterling silver letter opener.

She picked it up, amused by the figure of a stern face that was worked into the hilt. As she turned the lovely object slowly, enjoying the well-worn feel of fine silver, a sound of movement came from behind her.

"You disappoint me, Diana."

She froze, her skin suddenly cold, her heart thumping. Slowly her fingers curled around the letter opener in her hand, clutching at it as though it would save her from having to face him.

"I expected you to appear on my doorstep last night. Or at least to be waiting for me when I arrived here at the office this morning. What took you so long?"

She turned slowly. "I probably shouldn't have come at all," she said softly, watching him with a steady gaze.

His eyes glittered with a mocking amusement that inflamed her anger. His dark business suit was impeccably cut, with razor-sharp creases, and his crisp white shirt contrasted with the darkly tanned skin of his neck. He was all assurance, power, and arrogance. Her fingers tightened on the silver blade she still held in her hand.

"But, Diana," he said softly, watching her reaction with the enjoyment of a true connoisseur of discomfiture, "I was sure you would want to come in person so that we could talk over the old days."

She shook her head slowly. "I didn't come for that," she answered evenly.

"Oh?" His eyes pierced her, searching for the truth she was trying so desperately to hide.

Just then the door burst open and the secretary flew into the room. "Oh, Mr. Stuart!" she exclaimed. "I'm so sorry. She must have slipped by me when those tenants from the Nordon Building..." The woman's eyes suddenly rounded in shock as her gaze fell on the blade in Diana's hand. "Oh!" she gasped.

James Stuart smiled. "Don't worry, Mrs. Endicott. I was expecting a visit from Miss Kingston. Would you mind serving us some coffee?"

"But..." The frazzled woman pointed toward the letter opener Diana still held like a protective weapon.

"Miss Kingston may wish me dead, Mrs. Endicott," he said chuckling, "but she won't try it that way. Will you, Diana?"

His voice was like the purr of a large jungle cat, and his body moved with feline grace as he stepped forward to take the blade from her hand.

Of course Diana had no intention of using the weapon. She had never entertained any such notion. But she was bound and determined not to give in to this man in any way if she could help it, and she refused to loosen her grip on the letter opener now.

His fingers closed around her wrist, and he looked back at his secretary. "The coffee?"

Mrs. Endicott nodded, her eyes still wide with astonishment at these strange goings on, and she backed out of the room.

"Now, Diana," he said softly, looking down into her violet-blue eyes, "drop it."

"Make me," she answered childishly through clenched teeth, but she knew the game was up. His long, sinewy

Sweeter Than Wine 39

fingers seemed to burn against her skin, and the raw, male essence he exuded was suffocating her, drowning her in a sea of memories of how it once had been.

"Drop it," he said again, and though his fingers did not move to force the issue, his face was nearer to her own, nearer and descending, so that she knew what would happen if she didn't obey.

"No," she whispered, and for some reason her lips remained parted with the word, so that when his mouth swooped down to claim them, there was no barrier to his possession of the whole of her warm, sensitive mouth.

The shame of her response swept over her before he had finished the kiss. The sweet, narcotic effect he had on her was the same today as it had been six years ago. There was no use in denying its potency. But she had to fight it.

"Drop it, Diana," he murmured against the soft skin of her cheek as he rubbed his face against hers. "Drop it, or I'm going to have to punish you further, and Mrs. Endicott is going to be quite shocked at what she finds when she returns with the coffee."

She had no doubt that he was ready to back up his threat. She knew he could easily take the weapon from her if he chose. But he preferred to demonstrate that his power over her went beyond superior physical strength.

Yet it wasn't his words that finally gave her the will to pull away, but rather her own repulsion at how she had let this happen. Here she was letting him pull her back into the vortex, putting up no resistance, letting him see that his ascendancy over her was still as strong as it had ever been.

"You bastard!" she spat out as she tore herself from his grasp, throwing the letter opener down on the desk with a clatter. "Don't you ever dare touch me like that again!"

"Oh I'll dare, Diana." He chuckled as he dropped

down into his chair behind the desk. He leaned back, his eyes half-closed as he watched her.

Just then the door flew open, and the secretary entered with a tray. Diana sank slowly down into the chair facing James. When the matronly woman had left, she spoke again, but this time she was more in control of her emotions.

"Will you please explain to me what this name change is all about?" she said sharply. "Why are you now James Stuart when you were once Jamie Morel?"

"Interesting, isn't it?" he drawled, grinning good-naturedly. "A convenient device, changing names. People do count on them so much when they're trying to pigeonhole your character." He cocked an eyebrow at her. "As James Stuart I can do anything I please. For Jamie Morel life wasn't quite so easy."

Did he really think that constituted an explanation? "You'll have to explain more fully than that," she said icily.

He sighed, a consummate picture of the patient man sorely tried. "Very well. I have always been James Stuart. At the time I knew you, my parents had recently divorced and I was going through a period of youthful rebellion. I decided to go under my mother's maiden name." He shrugged. "And that's all there was to it."

Diana stared at him, perplexed. "But what made you go back to using your father's name?" she asked.

He looked down at his hands, extended on the desk before him, and she had a strange feeling that he was avoiding her eyes. But she shook that thought away. He was the aggressor. Why would he be wary of facing her?

"I realized that I was James Stuart, that I couldn't run away from it. And when my father asked me to join him in business, I agreed." He shifted restlessly in the seat. "I must admit that the work suits me better. I seem to be a natural at it."

"Why didn't you tell me?" she asked. "Why did you leave me to think you were just a field worker?"

His smile was cold and deadly as he finished the sentence for her. "A field worker who would not be welcome in the Kingston drawing room, someone you had to sneak out to meet in the night." His look of contempt stung, but she wouldn't let him see that. "But that's exactly what I was. And that was exactly what attracted you. Yes, Diana, I remember it well."

He leaned toward her across the desk. "Do you remember?" he asked softly, his blue eyes mesmerizing her with the intensity of his gaze. "Do you remember the first time you climbed up on Lion Mesa to visit me under the full moon?"

Involuntarily, memory flooded back. She had been so nervous. For three days after the incident with her car in the fields, she had tried to get up enough nerve to visit his camp as he had invited her to do. Finally her parents had left for a late party on Saturday night, and her chance had come. She had driven her sports car to a small grove where she could hide it from the road. Then she had struck out on foot. The light from his campfire had flickered against the dark purple sky, and the sound of his guitar had filled the night air, enhanced, as she drew nearer, by the warm sound of his fine baritone singing voice.

He had looked up as she approached, but he hadn't stopped playing the soft folk song. She had sat a good six feet away from him, her legs in their well-worn jeans crossed before her. And there she had stayed. They had talked. He had played folk songs for her, and then a love song or two, and finally he had touched her heart with a haunting gypsy tune that he said he had learned from his mother's people.

"Your mother is a gypsy?" she had asked, and he had nodded, his eyes dark and brooding in the firelight.

She had listened to his music and had watched him as he sang, and feelings such as she had not known existed had flooded through her in continuous waves. But he hadn't touched her. Not that night.

As the summer drifted lazily by, she had found more and more chances to slip away and join him in his lonely camp. By day she played tennis with Lawrence Farlow and, under her mother's urging, even dated him often in the evenings. But once she had told the Yale graduate good night, she had searched frantically for a chance to run out into the hills to meet her gypsy field worker.

She looked into that man's eyes, trying to see what he had once been, and was overwhelmed by the reality of what he was now.

"I don't remember a thing," she claimed stiffly.

"I do." His blue eyes darkened as he gazed at her until they looked as black as the lashes that rimmed them. As his dark gaze raked her body, she became self-concious about the rounded, thrusting breasts that jutted beneath her jersey dress. "I remember it well," he said softly. "I remember how jumpy you were at first, how you looked over your shoulder at every sound." He smiled, seemingly in spite of himself.

"But the music soothed you." He leaned back again in his chair, but his eyes never left her. "You especially liked the gypsy songs. I could see your pulse begin to quicken as you listened to the passion in those ancient tunes."

His voice was low now, and rasping in a sensual way that seemed to pull her near the hypnotizing power of him once again. She felt her body respond, her defenses deadened, her senses fully alive.

"I remember how you looked that night in the moonlight, your skin so pearly white. Do you remember, Diana? Do you remember how it was with us?"

Of course she remembered. The night had lived on

Sweeter Than Wine

in her dreams for years. How rash she had been. How insanely in love.

The summer had been almost over. Harvest time was near, just as it was today. Night after night she had come to visit him, and never once had he so much as kissed her. It began to rankle, the enforced separation he maintained. She began to wonder why he didn't seem to want her touch as she wanted his. She was fighting off Lawrence Farlow every night, but the man she now knew that she loved had never made a move toward her.

The idyll was almost over. In another week she was scheduled to begin her freshman year at a college a thousand miles away. A feeling of despair began to grow in her. She couldn't leave him. She knew she loved him. There had to be some way to stay together.

One early fall night, as they sat in the glow of the flickering firelight, she had asked him to teach her to play the guitar. The warmth of his fingers on her skin as he showed her the chording began to work its magic, and soon he laid the guitar aside and took her in his arms. He kissed her again and again, and then pulled away, telling her to leave.

"I want to stay," she whispered, her hands tangled in his thick hair, pulling his lips back toward her own. And then she boldly forced out, "I love you. I want to stay with you always."

The groan came from deep inside him as he twisted toward her. "I love you too, Diana," he admitted hoarsely.

"A forever kind of love?" she whispered, her lips caressing his ear.

"A forever kind of love," he breathed, pulling her body close against his.

"Prove it," she challenged.

And he had proved it. Once she had started that dangerous combustion, there had been no stopping it. His mouth on hers had lit a fire deep inside that she had not wanted to extinguish, even though she knew with terror what the result would be. As his hands had burned across her body, finding all the places where she hungered for his touch, she had thought the power was hers. She had been wrong.

She had been so young, and when he took her there in the moonlight, beside the campfire, she had been sure he was hers forever. So naive, she thought bitterly. So trusting.

"No," she stated flatly now. "I don't remember a thing. And I hope I never do."

He laughed then, and she knew her instincts had been right. As he threw back his head and roared his amusement, she knew she must never let him gain the advantage over her again.

She pushed her thick hair back from her flushed face and glared at him. "I want to know what you're after," she said evenly. "I want to know what this is all about."

His blue eyes were the picture of innocence. "Why, Diana," he said softly. "What do you think this is all about?"

She took a deep breath. "Do you really love my sister?"

The sparkle of his eyes conveyed more laughter. "Is there such a thing as real love?" he countered. "What do you think, Diana?"

"Of course there is," she replied stiffly, avoiding his eyes.

"Is there?" His voice was so low that she looked up quickly to see what his face could tell her. His gaze was blurred with memory again, and his soft voice went on, "Your hair was longer then, wasn't it? I remember it seemed almost to touch the back of your knees. And where the sunlight flashed across it there would be slashes of mellow silver in the black."

Sweeter Than Wine

She reached up to touch her hair, as though to hide it from his eyes.

"You looked like a princess to me," he almost whispered. "As you walked through the vineyards I thought of you as a princess walking out among her lowly subjects." His bright gaze shimmered over her. "Do you remember that day when we chased the blackbirds through the grapevines?" he asked, humor lilting through his voice. "We both ended up in the reservoir covered with mud."

She remembered. They had laughed so hard that she had thought they would drown. A tiny smile quivered between them as they both recalled that day.

Stop! shouted a warning deep inside Diana. Stop or he will catch you up in the past, and all your defenses will be torn down. Quickly, she looked away.

"Just like a princess," he repeated softly. Then his voice hardened. "And a princess never marries the pauper, does she?"

Diana's emotions were in chaos. In one breath he stirred memories that brought back the past so clearly. In the next he cut them to ribbons. What was he doing now? Trying to justify his behavior by pretending she had thought herself too good for him? It had never been like that, and he knew it.

"You haven't answered my question," she said shakily. "Why are you interested in Lisa?"

He raked her with a somber glance. "Why not?" he said shortly. "She's as good as the next one."

She ran her tongue over dry lips. "Why did you have to pick Lisa?"

He shrugged. "When I heard I was to meet the lovely Miss Kingston of Kingston Winery, I thought it would be you. I didn't even remember you had a sister. I was presented to Lisa instead, and we hit it off right away." He smiled with carefree cynicism. "I need to get married.

It's about time. And the Kingstons need an influx of capital, something I can provide. So why not merge our fortunes?"

Her throat was very dry. He didn't love Lisa at all. "You want the winery, don't you? And knowing that we had turned down every offer, you thought this was the only way you could get it!"

He didn't answer. To her surprise she seemed to detect a tremor of pain behind his hard glance, as though she had not guessed correctly at all, as though he had set out to get something very different. But, consumed with anger at his designs, she ignored that.

"You knew we would turn down cash, so you decided to use emotional blackmail. Isn't that so?"

His eyes darkened dangerously. "You can think what you want." His laugh was short and bitter. "Sure. Why not? I need your winery. It will merge so well with my other two, forming the biggest complex in the valley. And I'm willing to marry your sister to get it. That's what you believe, isn't it?"

Diana let her breath out in a long sigh. He had finally brought it out into the open. Now maybe she could fight it.

"I'll tell her," she rasped out. "I'll tell her all about us."

He leaned back and slowly shook his head, his eyes veiled in shadows, their expression unreadable. "Don't bother, Diana. I have a reputation for getting what I want. I've done the ground work. Your sister will marry me if that's what I decide I want."

She had to get out of this room, away from his influence, so that she could think clearly. Turning, she reached for the door, but found his dark hand covering hers before she could turn the knob.

"There's one more thing you should know," he said, his voice as hard as granite. He paused, and she waited, her heart beating a wild tattoo in her throat.

But he was shaking his head. "No," he said hoarsely. "It's been enough. But I'll see you this weekend. I'm really looking forward to my visit."

She stumbled out into the lobby in a numb haze. Vaguely she noticed the crowd of people still waiting to get in to see him. One man spoke as she passed.

"He's a bloody devil, isn't he?" the man said.

She made no response, but the name stuck with her. A bloody devil. That was exactly what he was.

CHAPTER
Four

"DON'T YOU WANT your change?"

The voice barely penetrated Diana's reverie, but she turned to find the coffee shop cashier holding out a handful of coins, and she groggily perceived that she was expected to take them from the woman.

"Thank you," she murmured, thrusting the clinking pieces of change into the pocket of her trench coat and continuing out the door into the chilly fog.

An atmosphere to match her mood, she thought, dredging up a small smile from somewhere deep inside her. Good old San Francisco always came through.

She had sat for the last hour in the steamy coffee shop, holding a mug of black coffee in her two hands, staring down into the murky depths and trying to work her way out of this mess.

She had to find a solution. There always was one, wasn't there? If she could just get it all straight in her mind.

She turned toward the rocky shore, welcoming the blanketing fog that reached out to pull her into its sheltering embrace.

"Better watch out, miss. That fog's thick as pea soup out there."

She flashed a smile at the fisherman who passed her on the walkway, but didn't change her direction. The fog felt like a friend today. The sun had been peeking through the clouds downtown, but she had come to the rocky coast in search of something else. She always turned to nature for her solace. The peace and continuity she found often soothed her, reassuring her that the world would go on despite her problems.

The sand scrunched beneath her leather boots, and she pulled her coat more tightly around her, following the sound of the lapping waves until she reached the water's edge. She made her way down toward the point where she knew from many a previous visit that the rocks were piled high and she would find a place to sit and think. All around her was a wall of thick, gray fog.

The boulder felt hard and rough beneath her hand, but she climbed up on it and stepped to the next and then the next, until she was well out on the point. There she found a stone that was flat enough to sit on, and she lowered herself to rest.

On a clear day the Golden Gate Bridge would have been clearly visible, as well as the wooded cliffs across the water. But today there was nothing but fog and the quiet, restful sounds of the bay.

It had been quite a different sort of day, that day when Jamie had betrayed her. The sun had been toasting the grass and the leaves to a late summer crisp, and she had worn a strapless sundress of white lace against her creamy golden skin, a party dress to wear to announce her engagement.

Her parents had been against it. When she had first come to them, blushing and hesitant, to announce that she was in love and wanted to get married, they had first thought she meant Lawrence Farlow. Even then they hadn't been pleased.

"You're too young," her mother had worried. "There's still college and all the fun of being single that you haven't experienced."

When she had explained that the man she loved was not Lawrence, that it was someone they didn't even properly know, they had dismissed the idea as an immature scheme.

"Forget about it, young lady," her father had ordered. "You're not marrying anyone, especially not someone we don't know."

Then she had been forced to endure a long lecture on her duty to the Kingston tradition, the honor of the Kingston name, the future of the winery. It was a message that had been drummed into her repeatedly through the years, and she barely listened, considering most of it old hat and hardly worth contemplating. She was young. She was in love. What did she care about such a mossy old heritage?

Her father was obviously still betting on Lawrence. The Farlows were involved in many lucrative ventures those days, but their heart was still in their winery holdings, and their antecedents in the Napa Valley went back even further than the Kingstons' did. Lawrence would be perfect in her father's eyes. Anyone else, especially some newcomer to the valley, was not to be considered.

Her father had not realized who Jamie was for the simple reason that she had not had the nerve to tell him.

But even if Jamie had been a college boy rather than a field worker, he would not have pleased her father. All sorts of naive plans had raced about in her head, plans to introduce Jamie as a stranger and hope that, dressed up, he would bear little resemblance to the man who worked for her father. Plans to elope, then present Jamie to them after the fact. Plans to elope and never look back. It had seemed so easy then.

She didn't know how she would do it; she only knew it must be done, for she could not live without him. And in the glory of their love, he seemed to feel the same.

"Diana, my darling," he groaned, his face hidden in her silky hair, her face pressed to his naked chest. "You're too young. I know you're much too young, but I can't bear to think of you cut off from me, away at college in a place I can't come near."

She had kissed his taut, smooth skin slowly, letting the wiry hair tickle her tongue. "Then marry me," she had demanded, thrusting her body at him in open persuasion. He had groaned, and she had felt the shudder of his desire rippling through his flesh.

"I'll do anything you want," he promised huskily. "Only stay against me like that. Don't ever move away."

She had told her parents that she wanted to get married. And they had all but laughed in her face. Scorn dripping from his tongue, her father had pretended it was just another childish lark. But she had planned her party, the traditional party she was allowed to hold for her friends at the end of every summer, not telling anyone what she was going to announce to the world, sure that when they met Jamie, when they saw how much in love the two of them were, her parents would give their consent.

It hadn't worked out that way. In the end it seemed that her parents were not the only ones laughing at her. Jamie was chuckling a bit as well. While she was dreaming of a honeymoon on the Mendocino coast and planning to surprise her parents and friends at her party, he was preparing his own surprise.

She had been so worried when he had not arrived as early as he had promised. All of her other guests had gathered, including Lawrence, who had waylaid her in the garden, trying to get a commitment from her. She had finally had to tell him the truth—that she was in love with someone else. In her anxiety, she had told everyone. All her friends had waited expectantly to see the man Diana wanted to marry.

When he walked in, dressed as though he had just come in from the fields, and with that girl, that horrible, voluptuous blonde who worked at the roadhouse where many of the younger field workers spent most of their pay, hanging on his arm, Diana did not believe her eyes. Jamie had faced her, his eyes blazing blue defiance, his mouth twisted into a cruel, hateful parody of a grin.

"Nice party, Diana," he drawled, pulling the scantily dressed girl closer against him. "Too bad we're going to have to miss it. Cherry and I are heading for Las Vegas. Wish us luck at the tables. And..." he grinned down at the blonde, who looked up, giggling into his face and clinging to him like a fleshy tropical vine, "...other things."

Everything seemed to come to a dead stop. The musicians had stopped playing, her friends had all stopped talking. All eyes and every attention had been focused on Diana and Jamie.

"Jamie," she rasped out, raw anguish twisting through her. "Is this your idea of a joke?"

His eyes glinted like polished diamonds, hard and sharpened to draw blood. "The only joke," he said through clenched teeth, "was this entire summer. And I'm going to laugh all the way to Vegas."

She had been suspended in some painful unreality,

a nether world of ghosts and goblins. Shadows feathered in around her vision, and sounds were contorted eerily. But she could see his eyes, his cruel blue eyes, flickering over Lawrence, who stood protectively by her side.

"Take good care of her, Larry," he said softly. "She's too spoiled to take care of herself."

Then his defiant glance swept across the room, treating everyone to his scorn. "All you little rich kids have yourself a good time," he sneered. "Have one hell of a good time. Have it on me."

And he turned on his heel, pulling Cherry with him.

Even after that Diana had not believed it. She had watched for one stunned moment, then run after him.

"Jamie!" she called, but he kept walking. "Jamie!" She caught him at the curve of the drive, pulling on his arm, forcing him to face her. "Jamie, please. I don't understand."

She was looking up into a stranger's face. The blue fire of his angry eyes reached out to burn her just as it had slashed at the others, and there was no love, no pity. She didn't know this hard, hateful man, and she let go of his arm.

"The summer is over, Diana," he said slowly, as though to a stubborn child. "You were a lot of laughs, but that's all it was."

"No," she whispered, still not believing it. "No."

His face darkened. "Grow up, Diana," he snarled. "You can't have it all."

Ignoring the simpering face that floated just beyond Jamie's shoulder, she still pleaded. "I don't want it all. I just want you."

His twisted grin was bitter. "You can't have me. But don't you worry, princess. Lover boy Larry is here to pick up the pieces." He threw an arm around Cherry, and without another word he was off down the drive.

Diana didn't remember much about the rest of the

party. Lawrence had seen her through it, that she knew. Dear Lawrence. He had made it very clear that he would stay if she would give him any hint that she might learn to love him in time. But that she could not give. She had loved once, and once was all for Diana.

It all came back so clearly now, as she sat upon her rock overlooking the fog-shrouded San Francisco Bay. The pain was still rapier-sharp. She had loved Jamie so wildly, so nakedly, and he had betrayed her so callously.

But why? That was a question she had never found the answer to. Had he really just been playing with her? Had she really been nothing to him but a summer pastime?

It had seemed so real. He had seemed so loving. As she thought now of the way they had lain together, she felt a hot flush rise to her cheeks, and she closed her eyes, fighting back the quivering surge that threatened to overwhelm her. God, but she had loved him! There would never be another like that for her. There would never be anyone for her. And she had James Stuart to thank for that.

Why had he done it? Had the whole thing been a means of revenge for some obscure slight, right from the beginning? A revenge that he still felt hadn't been fully realized? It didn't make any sense.

He had hurt her then, twisted her life into a knot she had still not unraveled. And now he was back, acting as though it was she who had wounded him, acting as though he still wanted revenge.

His revenge would lie in his marriage to her sister. Through her, he hoped to wrest control of the winery from Diana.

Perhaps that was all it was. After all, he had the reputation for being a ruthless businessman who would do just about anything to assure a victory. Perhaps he just wanted the winery.

She threw back her head and closed her eyes. If he only knew, she thought. The revenge he seemed to hunger for was already his. In coming back he had reopened the wound. And he had done something more. He had shaken her confidence. Now that she had seen him again, she was more afraid than ever of her own emotions. She thought she had developed her hatred of him into a solid wall of defense. Now it appeared that wall was riddled with weakness.

But sitting here wasn't going to get anything accomplished. With renewed energy she vaulted down off the rocks and strode back across the sand. She could think until doomsday and still not find the answer to the puzzle she had been working on for six years. There was no point in wasting any more time on it. She must move and move fast if she was to parry his latest thrust.

She must get to Lisa. She had wasted too much time already. Once Lisa knew some of the background, Diana was sure her sister would see things her way.

Driving back along the coast, Diana's spirits grew lighter by the minute. Lisa would listen to reason. No man had ever meant so much to her that she would be ready throw caution to the winds and follow her impulses. She had been in and out of love a dozen times in the last few years. Surely she could fall out of love again.

The apartment house where Lisa lived was large and modern, a glistening white multistoried building studded with balconies dripping with jungle greenery. Diana parked in the basement lot and took an elevator to her sister's floor.

"Diana! I can't believe it! What could have possibly lured you away from the country?" Lisa laughed into her sister's face with sincere delight.

He hadn't called yet, Diana told herself with relief. It would still make a difference if she told the truth.

"I've got something serious to talk to you about," she

announced, turning to look out the huge, floor-to-ceiling window at the lovely view of the city.

Lisa frowned upon hearing the emotion in Diana's voice. "Let me take your coat," she said quietly, "and we'll have a cup of tea."

"No!" Diana turned to her sister. "No tea. This is going to be hard for me, Lisa, and I want to get it over with quickly. Please sit down and listen to what I have to say."

Lisa's blue eyes became clouded with bewilderment. "Of course," she said softly. "Come sit by me."

They sat together on the sectional sofa that curved about one entire side of the room. Diana reached out and took Lisa's hand, holding it tightly. She looked searchingly into the clear blue eyes, wondering how she could tell Lisa in a way that would cause the least pain.

"It's about James Stuart," she began haltingly. But before she could get out another word, Lisa took up the slack.

"Oh, Diana! What did you think? Isn't he wonderful? He's just the kind of man you dream about when you're just starting to date, the kind you soon cease to to believe in as you meet dull, boring man after dull, boring man. The more I'm with him, the more I realize just how perfect we are for each other. Why, if—"

"Lisa!" Diana could stand no more. "You can't marry him!"

The sparkling eyes widened in amazement. "What on earth are you—?"

"That's what I came to tell you. He's...James and I knew one another before. He's...you can't marry him."

"You and James?" Lisa's look of amused incredulity stung Diana. "I don't believe it!"

Diana dropped her sister's hand and glared at her. "What do you think I'm doing, making it up?"

Lisa laid a placating hand on Diana's arm. "No, darling, of course not. But... you and James?" She stifled a giggle that did nothing to mollify her sister. "When did this happen?"

Diana took a deep breath. "Do you remember the summer you were sixteen, when Aunt Margery took you with her family to Europe and I stayed home because—"

"Because you had gone the year before. Certainly I remember." She frowned. "You met James that summer?"

Diana nodded. "He was a field worker."

"What?" Lisa's laugh pealed out through the elegantly furnished room. "I don't believe it!"

Ignoring her, Diana went on. "We met and... dated." Dated was hardly the word for it, but how else could she put it?

"Daddy let you go out with a field hand?" Lisa seemed to find it more and more amusing.

"Of course not. I... we met out on Lion Mesa."

"Diana!" Lisa's eyes were shining with patronizing love. "How cute! Why didn't you ever tell me?" She grinned mischievously. "What other secrets are you hiding away under that serious demeanor? I had no idea you ever had such a romantic encounter."

Diana stared anxiously at her sister. This wasn't turning out as she had planned. She would have to be more frank. But just how much could she tell? How much could she live with once it was out in the open?

"Lisa, please, this is serious. It wasn't just an encounter. It was much more than that."

Lisa bounced excitedly on the sofa, her eyes glowing with delight. "Your first love, right? Oh, Diana, I'm so glad. What better man to have that with than James? He was younger then, but I bet he was just as sexy, wasn't he?"

Diana frowned. "Doesn't it bother you?" she demanded.

Lisa's laugh trilled through the room. "Of course not! Why should it? Oh, Diana, you're so naive! If you'd only run around with the crowd I've been hanging out with all these years you'd know that we're always trading off escorts. Life is too short to get upset about a thing like old loves. A man like James must have had tons of them. So what? Live for today, I always say."

She meant it, too; Diana could see it plainly. Stunned, she groped for a new tack.

"He's going to take the winery away from me," she said.

Lisa's eyes twinkled. "Now, what ever gave you that idea?"

"He said so. I've just been to see him at his office. He said he wants the winery."

Lisa sighed. "Diana, don't worry. I know how much the winery means to you. I'll take care of it. Just give me time—I'll have him eating out of my hand. Don't I always?"

Diana shook her head. "Not this time. James won't eat out of anyone's hand."

Lisa shrugged her delicate shoulders. "Okay, listen. If it will make you feel any better, we'll get it out into the open right now. He'll be here in just a few minutes for our dinner date. If you just stay—"

"No!" Diana rose, hugging her coat in closer around her. "I don't want to see him."

"Oh, Diana." Lisa's voice showed her exasperation.

"No." She walked quickly to the door of the apartment. "You talk to him, see what you think. I'll call you tomorrow."

She was out the door and down the corridor before her sister could utter another word. She and Lisa lived by different codes. She had always known that, but never before had it been shown to her quite so eloquently. She had as good as told her sister that she and James had been lovers, yet Lisa didn't care. If it were the other way around, if Lisa were sleeping with James.... She couldn't hold that thought, for it tore a jagged, ripping wound through her chest, and her breath came out in a moan.

She hurried to her car, not wanting to intercept James on her way. Stepping off the elevator, she walked quickly toward the Triumph, glancing back over her shoulder as she reached out to open the door. But before she had pulled the door fully open, a deep, rich voice stopped her.

"Hello, Diana."

He was sitting in the passenger's seat, and she stood for a moment, steeling herself for another encounter. Should she leave? Should she run back to Lisa's apartment?

No. She would face him. She slipped down into the seat next to the man she had been trying to avoid.

"What are you doing here?" she whispered, trying to control her racing pulse. He was so large, so powerful, that the force of his personality seemed to fill the little car, leaving only a tiny corner for her to squeeze into.

"Waiting for you." His brilliant blue gaze played over the line of her lips, then he glanced at her eyes and began a slow, heavy-lidded examination of her temple, her ear, the curve of her cheek. One hand reached out to trail across the tousled ends of her blue-black hair. "You ought to thank me. I saw your car and decided to let you have your say with Lisa without my interference. Wasn't that gentlemanly of me?"

She could hardly think. There was too much of him too close. She seemed to breathe in his scent with every breath, and it was clean and masculine and caused her fingers to curl convulsively into tight fists. "You don't know what it means to be a gentleman," she forced out harshly.

"Yes." His smile was bitter. "That's the point, isn't it?" His fingers tangled in her hair, tugging slightly. "And how did it go? Did you convince your sister to drop me like the low-down wretch that I am?"

She lowered her eyes, staring at the steering wheel. "No," she whispered, wishing she could despise him, hating his answering chuckle.

"I didn't think it would work," he said, amusement tinting his tone. "It'll be interesting to see how she acts toward me now."

Fury blazed up in Diana. "What is this, some sort of experiment?" she asked angrily. "Are you going to poke and prod us to see how we react to your stimuli?"

"What an enticing suggestion," he answered sensually, his eyes skimming the lines of her neck. "I'll see if we can fit that into my plans."

"And just what are your plans, Mr. James Stuart? Besides marrying a woman you don't love and stealing my winery from me, just what are your plans?"

He added a twist to the hair around his fingers and gave it another little tug. "My plans are my business, princess. Haven't you ever heard the old expression 'loose lips sink ships'?"

"That was during the war."

"And what is this, Diana?" His voice was suddenly harsh and cold, and his hand wound more tightly around her hair to hold her head prisoner. "I've been at war with you for a long, long while. It's about time we had a decisive battle and declared a victor."

His eyes were fiery, blazing like stars in the gloomy interior of the car. Diana felt a quiver of terror shake her body, and she knew he felt it too. His smile was bemused. Slowly, very slowly, he forced her face toward his. Just fractions of an inch away from her, he stopped, his eyes glaring into hers, his breath hot on her lips. "Kiss me," he ordered harshly.

She tried to draw away, but his ruthless hand only gripped her hair tightly.

"Kiss me like you used to when we were lovers, Diana." Then the harshness faded, and in its place she suddenly saw a lightning flash of pain, a vulnerability that made her want to reach out to him, to take away whatever was hurting him. He had been so dear to her. Could that loved one still be hiding behind this cold facade? She had to find out.

Slowly she moved toward him, pressing her cool lips to his warm ones. She kissed him gently, almost lovingly. She kissed him, but his lips were hard and unyielding, wanting no part of her, humiliating her. He wanted no kiss; he wanted only tribute.

Repelled, she began to pull away. But as she did, a groan rumbled deep in his throat and then he *was* kissing her, giving away the game, delivering himself to her in a gesture that held more than anger, more even than desire. Did she dare compare it to what she had known with him before?

He was drawing away again. She let him go, trying to read some clue in his wary expression.

"Why?" she whispered.

His laugh was low and cynical. "Why? Because I wanted you to feel what it's like to be rejected."

She didn't know what he meant, but he had misread her question. "No," she said softly. "Why do you hate me so?"

He pulled his hand away, and it seemed that he shrank a bit, drawing himself up into his side of the car and away from her. His eyes were tremendous. He didn't answer her.

"Same old car," he said instead. "Remember how we

rode all over the dusty hills in this thing?"

She remembered. She remembered too much. Shaking her head, she said, "What do you want with me?"

He shifted restlessly, avoiding her eyes. "Whatever happened to that guy you were cheating on when you came out to visit me on Lion Mesa?" he asked gruffly.

"I don't know what you're talking about." Her indignant voice seemed to amuse him.

"You know who I mean. Lawrence Farlow. Good old Larry."

"He lives in New York. He's a broker with his uncle's investment firm on Wall Street."

There was a long silence. Finally he went on. "What happened to the romance between you two?"

She looked at him sharply. "Romance? There was no romance between me and Lawrence."

He turned toward her again, and the air between them crackled with the intensity of his stare. "You know," he said so softly, so thinly, that it was almost no more than a passing breeze, "I think I could stand it better if I thought you had been in love with him."

She had no idea what he was driving at, but she had been through enough for one day. With all her heart she wanted to be free of him, to rest in her own bed, to sleep and forget about James Stuart for just a few hours. Leaning back, she closed her eyes and waited for him to finish with her.

"So you let Larry slip through your fingers. And in all these years you never found any one else to marry? What was wrong, Diana? Or was it just a case of 'ordinary mortals need not apply'? Not too many bluebloods like Larry around, are there?"

"Would you please get out of my car and let me go?"

"Why, Diana?" he asked in a voice that was almost teasing. "You never asked me to leave before." He moved closer to her, catching her chin in his large, strong hand. "Whatever else you may have thought of me, you always did like this."

His mouth was warm and silky smooth on her lips, and she couldn't help but respond. His seduction was gentle, teasing, his teeth softly nipping at her lips, his tongue searching for every sweet drop of honey she might harbor. She sighed as she turned toward him like a flower to the sun. He was right. She always had liked that. Once she had thought she couldn't live without it. But she had cured herself of that addiction. Was she going to have to go through that all over again?

"Oh, Diana," he breathed against her swollen lips. "Why didn't you have a little more faith?" He rose beside her, looking down into her face with haunted eyes. "I can't believe you didn't love me. Tell me that you did."

She gazed at him, bewildered. Of course she had loved him. He knew that. Why did he pretend to have doubts?

"Never mind." He turned roughly and opened the door. She stared after him in silence as he unfolded his long body from the little car and stood beside it, bending down to talk to her through the low doorway.

"I'll see you this weekend, Diana."

With a slam of the door that rang in her ears, he was striding toward the elevator, striding toward his date with Lisa.

CHAPTER
Five

AFTER DRIVING ONLY two blocks, Diana knew she would have to pull over and get herself together before attempting the long trip home. Her hands were shaking as she brought the car to a stop in a parking spot next to a busy department store. Turning off the engine, she leaned forward against the steering wheel, her eyes closed, feeling her pulse race.

She still loved James. That was as clear to her as the sound of the traffic on the street. If he had stayed away, she would have done very nicely with her life. But he had put himself back in it, and now things weren't going to be so easy.

He had loved her once. The memories he recalled reaffirmed that. And he held those memories dear. She smiled to herself as she thought of his face when he had recited them for her. Yes, he had loved her as much as she had loved him.

But something had killed that love. What could it be? The question haunted her. He was like a man seeking revenge, but what did he resent in their past? She hadn't left; she hadn't betrayed him.

She remembered how he had spoken of Lawrence. Did James think she had been more serious about Lawrence than she had been? Had jealousy poisoned their love?

The theory didn't hold together. He had known about her dates with Lawrence, known she went out with him only to please her parents, to put up a smoke screen so that they wouldn't suspect about her relationship with Jamie. It hadn't seemed to bother him at the time. Why should he act now as though it did?

But even if he had been jealous of Lawrence, that didn't explain the way he had left her. A jealous man might have insisted on a confrontation, but he wouldn't simply walk out, giving the prize away without a fight. That wasn't the style James Stuart was known for.

He didn't love Lisa. And she was fairly sure Lisa didn't love him. The two of them were playing a game, each for his own separate reasons. Was the winery the prize?

A shiver ran through her as she thought of the way he had made her kiss his bitter, unresponsive lips. That had been the act of a vengeful man. Who knew what other things he would demand of her.

The drive home was uneventful. She felt again the thrill of turning up the drive and seeing the medieval-looking, ivy-covered winery and the adjacent house, both built of limestone quarried from the nearby mountains and hauled through the valley, both looking old and comfortable and able to last, the antithesis of the modern age of sleek disposabality. Old-fashioned. That was what her winery was. Old-fashioned in appearance, old-fashioned in goals and principles. Diana loved it that way.

"Diana!"

She sighed as she saw Gunther bounding toward her across the lawn. Stepping from her Triumph, she began walking wearily toward the house, sure that the vintner would meet her at her front door.

"Where have you been all day?" he scolded as he came to a stop before her. Gunther was always in a hurry, and the disjointed parts of his lanky body never seemed to arrive all at once.

She forced a smile to her lips. "I had business in the city. Why? Has something happened?"

"I wanted to let you know that I will be gone this weekend. Gregor at the university has been doing some experiments I want to take a look at. We might be able to apply them to our ruby cabernet." He shifted his weight restlessly. "Oh, and I've got to run some damaged barrels over to the cooper for restoring. I can do that on my way."

She stared at him, feeling a tiny thread of panic. "Oh, not this weekend, Gunther! You can't!"

He frowned in annoyance. "Of course I can. Don't be silly. I'm a free man. You don't own every minute of my life." Gunther sometimes tended toward the dramatic, but long association had taught Diana to disregard his hyperboles.

She caught her lower lip between her teeth. The vintner wasn't the ideal protector, but she needed someone to help her get through James's visit. "Gunther, please stay home this weekend," she pleaded. "We're having a male guest, and I'd feel better if you were here."

His look of disgust made her smile despite her worries. "A male guest. And what am I to be? A chaperon? No thank you!"

"This is special, Gunther. This is the man who might be marrying Lisa."

Gunther's head swung up, his eyes wide with shock that was exaggerated by his thick glasses. "Marrying Lisa?" he choked out. The word that followed was in German, but Diana thought it must be a curse from the sound of it. "Who is this man?" he demanded angrily.

Gunther's reaction didn't surprise her. He'd had a crush on her sister for years—just like every other man. She had never considered it any more serious than that.

"James Stuart," she said simply, wondering if Gunther had heard about James's interest in the winery. She quickly found out he had.

"What? A man like that?... Diana, we cannot let Lisa throw herself away on such a man. Oh, mein Gott!" Diana could see that he was considering the other complications. "My winery!" he wailed. "We can't let him get his hands on my winery."

"*My* winery," Diana reminded him dryly. "And that is just the point. I need you here to help me."

"Help you! I'll do anything. Tell me what you plan. Shall I tell him to leave the area? Shall I challenge him? I still have my dueling swords. Shall I fight him with my fists?"

Diana suppressed a smile as she pictured the slightly built, sinewy man coming up against the powerful figure of James Stuart, but she was touched by his loyalty. His pale blue eyes were full of fury, and she knew she could count on him to back her up.

"No." She beamed at him. "No fighting. Just be around. Come to dinner Friday night, and we'll take it from there."

As she started to turn toward the house, she felt his hand on her arm. Startled, she looked up into his face.

"Is she really going to marry him?" he asked desolately.

Sweeter Than Wine 69

Diana's smile held more reassurance than she felt. "Not if we can help it," she said firmly. He would have to be satisfied with that. At least for the time being.

The faces around the table were shadowed by the flickering candlelight.

"Tell me, Mr. Stuart," Gunther cut into the conversation, his tone accusatory, his eyes glinting angrily. "Now that you have ravaged half the neighborhood, is it your intention to rape Kingston Winery as well?"

Lisa gasped at Gunther's rudeness, her lovely blue eyes wide with dismay, but James only smiled, leaning back in his chair, the picture of a man totally at his ease.

"It certainly sounds as though you and Diana have been talking," he mused quietly, his voice and manner expressing supreme self-confidence. "And she has already made it quite clear that she thinks I am a despoiler. But rape is an ugly word, Mr. Werner, whether talking about a winery or a woman. I have never violated either one, and I don't intend to begin now."

Gunther snorted. "Well, what do you call what is happening at the Rio de Oro Winery? They had a nice little Chablis, a distinctive flavor that deserved developing. Now that you have taken the place over, I hear they are shifting to something called sparkling picnic wines." He glared at the darker man. "Is that true, or have I perhaps slandered you?"

James's wide mouth twisted with amusement. "Your information is absolutely correct, Mr. Werner. We are working on something light, something any young couple might take along on a trip to the seashore with their peanut butter sandwiches. In fact, I just signed a contract with Merter Advertising today. We plan massive television promotion beginning this winter."

Gunther pouted in disgust. "Television advertising," he muttered, horrified. "Just like mouthwash. But that's all a wine like that deserves."

"You know," James said dryly, tongue firmly in cheek, "that's an angle I hadn't thought of. Remind me to mention it to the advertising people."

Diana found herself smiling, but the amusement quickly left her eyes when they met James's from across the table. He had been in her house for barely an hour, and already she felt as though he had usurped her possession of it.

James and Lisa had swept in like a pair of city sophisticates come to patronize the country folk. Diana had taken pains with her appearance, brushing her hair until it curled about her shoulders in gleaming waves. She wore a floor-length, persimmon-colored gown that was cut low at the neckline and even lower at the back, leaving it totally bare to the base of her spine. It was made of a slinky fabric that hugged the lines of her body, revealing every curve. She had urged Gunther to dress well too, helping him pick out a nicely cut blue suit instead of the jeans and fisherman's sweater he would rather have worn.

But Lisa and James put them both to shame. Lisa was shimmering in a creation of blue and silver that seemed almost transparent, barely a misty film of light and movement that hovered about her beautiful form and set off the cloud of golden hair that framed her lovely face. Diana had felt the bitter taste of envy rise in her throat the minute her sister had walked in the door.

Don't be silly, she had told herself. This wasn't a competition. But she had felt the jealousy just the same.

Especially when she had turned to welcome James. His black slacks emphasized the long, supple length of his legs, and the creamy white of his dinner jacket set off his tan skin and his startlingly blue eyes so that she could hardly keep from staring at him. Whatever else

James had become, he was still the most handsome and desirable man she had ever seen.

"Just get off your high horse, Gunther," Lisa was sputtering indignantly. "Just stick to what you know best and leave the larger concerns to James. He knows what he's doing."

There had always been a cheerful antagonism between Lisa and the vintner, ever since he had come to work for them two years ago, just before their father died. Their squabbling often reminded Diana of a couple of feisty puppies. But right now Lisa was sincerely angry as she defended James.

Diana noticed that no one had spoken of the most important issue—was there going to be a wedding? Lisa and James had made no formal announcement, and Diana hadn't had a chance to speak to Lisa alone since the afternoon she had told her about her past relationship with James. The way the two of them acted gave rise to lots of questions. Though they exchanged smiles occasionally, Diana couldn't help but notice that James's eyes were on her rather than on Lisa. At the same time Lisa seemed to enjoy baiting Gunther more than flirting with the man she claimed she intended to marry.

But she had made it clear to Diana that James would soon join the family. "Oh, sit at the head of the table, James," Lisa had said when they'd come out to the terrace to dine at the marble table set among the hanging plants and potted orange trees. He had looked for all the world like the lord of the manor, calmly surveying the gleaming silver place settings laid out on the flawless white linen, all glittering in the candlelight. Gazing at him, Diana felt a stabbing pang. He looked so right there. Was he already the master in all but official name?

"This is such a wonderful old place," he was saying now. "A castle fit for a princess."

Diana's startled gaze met his, and she found it surprisingly warm. Watch out, her alarm system warned. Don't let down your defenses.

"When was it built?" he went on, still studying her.

"The winery was built first," Diana answered coolly, trying to pretend that her heart wasn't beating faster at the caressing quality of his voice. "In eighteen eighty-nine. But of course the original vineyards were planted fifteen years before that. The owners worked in sheds until the limestone structure could be completed. And once that was done, they began to build the house."

"These were ancestors of yours, weren't they?"

She nodded. "Yes. Our great-grandfather."

"And the Kingston Winery still prevails," he mused quietly. "Quite a heritage."

"Yes." She flashed him a sizzling look. "Through wars and Prohibition, when they were forced to dump half the harvest and sell the rest for raisins, through the Great Depression and the Second World War, they prevailed." She let her challenging glare show plainly what she only thought: *And we'll endure even you, James Stuart*.

His eyes gleamed, though she couldn't tell if it was with amusement or anger at her implications. "My own heritage is much less savory," he announced wryly. "My grandfather made his living by cheating people out of their land. He got rich and married well, and the family quickly pretended that class just naturally came with the money. But somehow it never rang true." He cast a buccaneering grin about the table. "I guess I take after the old man, wouldn't you say?"

"Undoubtedly," Diana grated out, but Lisa hushed her.

"You're a perfectly lovely man, and you know it," she admonished him firmly, though with a teasing pout.

Sweeter Than Wine 73

"Now talk nicely, or we'll make you leave the table."

Diana would have liked to see Lisa try to make James do anything he didn't want to do, but she kept her peace, and soon he was speaking again.

"Tell me about your parents," he said softly to Lisa. "I remember them both from my summer working in your vineyard."

Swallowing a lump in her throat, Diana was glad he had not asked the question of her.

"Well, Mother slipped away from us almost three years ago." Diana found her sister's description rather apt. Their mother had never been a forceful person, and though they had loved her, her passing had been as quiet as her life. The surprising thing had been the effect it had upon their father.

"Her death broke Daddy's heart. Within six months he was gone too."

"What a shame," James murmured. "He was still a relatively young man."

"Yes," Lisa answered sadly. "But he seemed to give up when Mother died. He knew he was going."

"It must have worried him to leave the two of you, with both of you unmarried and unprotected." James's voice was sympathetic, but Diana caught an ironic glint in his eyes.

"Oh no." Lisa laughed. "He knew I would finally settle down with someone perfect." She smiled impishly up into his face. "And of course he was right. And he knew Diana would take good care of the winery." She laughed again. "After she refused to marry Lawrence Farlow, he gave up on her ever marrying."

Diana felt James's gaze burning into her, and lifting her eyes, she met his slight frown.

"Did you meet Lawrence, James?" Lisa asked. "That summer you worked here?" It seemed that the past was of so little importance to Lisa that she could toss it idly into the conversation. "He kept after Diana for two years, but he never could wear her down. Finally he gave up and married some Wellesley girl from Boston."

Lisa babbled on, but Diana had the feeling that James wasn't hearing a word of it. Whenever she looked up, her gaze tangled with his darkened, clouded eyes. They brooded at her from across the flickering candlelight, burrowing into her soul, and she felt desperate to escape from his probing.

"Tell us about your parents, James," she said suddenly. "Your mother was a gypsy, wasn't she? Isn't that what you once told me?" She hoped her question would make him think about something other than his examination of her, and for once, it worked.

His eyes were shadowed, but she could see by the softness that came over his face that he had warm feelings for his mother.

"Yes," he said slowly. "Her people were gypsies from Romania. Although she was born in this country, she retains a great deal of the heritage."

"And your father?" Diana asked curiously. Why hadn't she delved into this subject that summer six years ago?

He took a deep breath. "My father ran Stuart Enterprises until his death five years ago. I run it now."

She could tell he didn't want to talk about his father, and she remembered he had said that his parents were divorced. Suddenly she recalled what Millie had said about an unhappy mystery in his father's past.

"So your mother was a gypsy!" Lisa cooed. "How exciting. Tell me all about your parents. How did they meet?"

Diana could see his hesitation, and quickly she broke in. "Lisa, James doesn't need to be interrogated..."

Sweeter Than Wine 75

But he was shaking his head, a smile of appreciation lighting his blue eyes. "Thanks, Diana," he said softly, "but I don't mind talking about it." His smile widened to include Lisa. "It's a rather romantic story, actually. The Stuarts were a rich and powerful family. Old San Francisco bluebloods on my grandmother's side. Rapacious nouveaux riches on my grandfather's. They were also very proud, and very aware of their station in life."

Diana wondered why his smile seemed to have developed a bitter edge.

"My mother is quite different," he went on. "I've already told you about her gypsy background. My father met her at the beach where she was working in a hotdog stand. It was love at first sight. He swept her off her feet, and they eloped within the week, totally against his family's wishes, of course. A modern Cinderella."

"How cute," Lisa bubbled. "And did they live happily ever after?"

"No." Abruptly his mood turned somber. "No, they did not." He turned toward Gunther, gesturing toward the crystal decanter. "More wine, Mr. Werner?"

Clearly he didn't want to talk any more about it, but Diana felt compelled to try one more question. "Where is your mother now?" she asked softly.

"My mother lives in an apartment in San Francisco," he said slowly, raising his glass so that the wine shimmered gold in the candlelight.

"Oh," Lisa cried, oblivious to his mood. "You never told me that. When do I get to meet her?"

He hesitated. "She's not well," he said at last, and Diana knew immediately that he was lying—at least shading the truth.

Deciding she would best help by changing the subject, she set aside her salad fork and assumed a conciliatory smile. "That was quite a siege you were under at your office the other day," she said lightly. "I thought those people were about to drag out the cannons and breech the walls. What had you done to make them so angry?"

His frown let her know immediately that she had made a bad choice of topics.

"Those people are tenants in a building that Stuart Enterprises has recently purchased. They feel that the fact that they live in the building gives them the right to chart the destiny of the structure." His lip twisted in annoyance. "We've offered them fair compensation, but they don't want to move out."

Lisa looked up with interest. "Are you talking about that tenant bunch? A group of them followed us into a restaurant last night, yelling and screaming like banshees. James had to have them dragged away."

Diana glanced at James, wondering at the picture of him having people dragged off like medieval squatters, but his sudden smile convinced her that Lisa was exaggerating.

The arrival of the entrée brought a welcome interruption, and for the rest of the meal Gunther held forth on the virtues of vegetarianism, all the while devouring the tasty dinner before him.

The meal of Cornish game hens and a wild rice dish was delicious, but Diana didn't taste a thing. Mrs. Cruz, the woman who came to clean twice a week, and to cook when Diana was entertaining, sniffed with disapproval when she arrived to clear away Diana's place.

"I'm sure I tried my best," she mumbled, ignoring the placating smile Diana threw her.

"It was wonderful," the others assured her, but somehow Diana's lack of enthusiasm seemed to mean more to the older woman than the others' praise.

"Let's take a walk in the garden," Lisa suggested, rising with an amused glance at Mrs. Cruz. The others readily agreed.

The night air was soft and seductive, and though the moon wasn't out yet, the star-studded sky provided ample illumination for them to see their way among the rose bushes.

"Look out at those vineyards," James said suddenly, standing at the clearing and gazing down over the valley, black and eerie in the darkness. "Just think of the wealth they contain."

"All you care about is money," Gunther began to sputter, but James silenced him with a short laugh.

"Money!" he barked in disgust. "What has money got to do with it?" He shook his head, and a strange, bemused smile curled his lips. "The magic in the grape. The mystery of the vintage. That's the wealth I'm talking about."

A chill tickled Diana's spine. The words he spoke might have come from her father's lips.

"When I worked in those fields," James went on, "I used to dream of what it would be like to own them, to have a hand in creating something of quality, something big and clean..." Suddenly he turned back toward the others, his grin almost shy, as though he hadn't meant to reveal so much of his inner thoughts.

"And of course I now have my own wineries," he said lightly. But Diana had heard more significance behind his words. The two other wineries he owned would produce inexpensive wine, but he would need Kingston Winery to provide quality vintage. He wanted the winery. She was sure of it.

They wandered here and there, talking softly. When Lisa and Gunther fell into an argument about the culture of three-year-old tea roses, Diana wasn't surprised that James left them behind and followed her down the path toward the carp pond.

She didn't realize he was behind her until his hand touched the nape of her neck, sweeping back the thick, black hair and softly stroking her naked skin.

She pulled away, turning on him angrily. "You may be able to fool my sister, James," she said bitingly, "but I know you don't really want her. I know what you're really after."

"Do you, Diana?" he whispered, his eyes huge and dark in the shadows. "And what do you think? Am I going to be successful?"

She raised her chin challengingly. "No!"

He frowned. "I had hoped for a more encouraging answer."

She laughed in astonishment. "You expect encouragement from me? You must be crazy!"

"Yes." His voice was broodingly low. "I think I am a little crazy. But it's all your fault, and you know it."

His hand was on her back again, touching the cool skin. She tried to pull away, but his fingers curled about her neck, holding it softly, persuasively.

"Look at me," he ordered, but she kept her head turned away, her eyes on the distant hills.

His finger began a slow descent along her spine, moving as gently as a rose petal floating on a breeze, but it created a choking flood of sensation that stunned her, caught at her breath, and quickened her pulse.

"Look at me," he whispered, his fingers sliding in under the edge of her low-backed gown and caressing the skin at the small of her back. Quivers of response spilled through her, tempting her to remember things best left in the past.

She turned quickly, gazing up into his shadowed eyes, her own begging him to stop the havoc he was rousing within her. "Don't," she pleaded huskily.

His eyes were devouring her parted lips and narrowing with intensity. "I'm going to kiss you, Diana," he stated harshly. "I've been watching that mouth for the last hour, anticipating how good it was going to taste. And I can't wait any longer."

Sweeter Than Wine

"No!" she cried out in panic. "They can see you."

With one swift movement he had pulled her behind the curve of the arbor from which fragrant yellow roses drooped. His kiss was short and savage, but it ignited a fire within her that Diana had hoped had been extinguished forever. The lips that released hers swept down the tender, sensitive line of her neck. James buried his face in her hair and breathed deeply of her scent.

"It's still there, isn't it, Diana?" His voice was almost triumphant in its mocking certainty. "That magic still works between us."

She couldn't deny it, but she lowered her eyes, unwilling to let him see just how right he was.

His large, strong hands slid down the sides of her slinky dress, curving over her hips and pulling her to him. "Why do you try to ignore it?" he asked huskily. "Why can't you see that you need me as much as I need you?"

"No," she protested weakly. Then, with more effort than she had ever exerted before, she pulled together the strength to tear herself away from him. Standing just out of his reach, she said more firmly, "No, James. You might as well know that I'm totally dedicated to fighting you on this. I'll do anything I can to keep you from getting what you want."

His reply was interrupted by the approach of the others, who could be heard just around the arbor. Diana stepped out to greet them. She was shaken by James's actions. There was no denying the desire that rose in her at his touch, no denying the way her heart beat faster when he was near, the way she still loved him. If Lisa and Gunther hadn't been present... but she was only thankful that they were, for she was beginning to realize how little defense she had against the advances James was mounting against her.

Luckily she was becoming more adept at hiding the

turmoil inside her. She was able to smile coolly and speak pleasantly, as though she were completely serene.

She led the party through the extensive gardens, showing off the sections that were still well-maintained, partly through her own efforts and partly through the efforts of the once-a-week gardener. It interested her how naturally Gunther took his place next to Lisa, while James invariably walked at her own side. She wondered if the others noticed it.

"We used to have a full-time gardener when we were kids." Lisa sighed with regret. "It was always so beautiful then."

"It wouldn't take long for a crew to get this all back into mint condition," James murmured speculatively, his eyes roaming over the weed-infested herb garden.

Lisa threw him a happy smile and agreed with a giggle. "Wouldn't it be wonderful to make this into a showcase again?"

Diana felt a lump rising in her throat. "The gardens aren't really important," she said with false calm, hiding her emotions with difficulty. "The winery must take all our energies right now. Gunther and I have no time for such frivolous things as gardens. Have we, Gunther?"

"No, indeed," he answered crisply, though his eyes still clung to Lisa's pretty face. "We're busy developing the best wine in this part of the valley, and we have no time for anything else."

James's lips quirked in amusement. "The wine we've been seeing from Kingston Winery is good, but it hardly ranks with the best," he scoffed, throwing a sly glance the vintner's way. "There are wines ten times better within a radius of twenty miles."

He couldn't have said anything more calculated to infuriate Gunther. "Is that right, Mr. Big Shot? Is that right?" His blue eyes were fierce, and the veins of his neck stood out prominently in his rage. "And who made you such an authority? What credentials do you claim?"

James smiled. "One hardly needs credentials to discriminate between greatness and mediocrity," he said softly.

"Just when was the last time you tasted our wine, James?" Diana asked sharply, also stung by his cynicism.

He gazed at her and shrugged. "A less than memorable wine does not linger on the memory," he said quietly.

"Then I think it only fair that you back up your insults with some hard evidence," she flashed back. "Gunther, bring some wines from the cellars."

"Of course." The vintner was confident of victory now. "I'll go immediately." Running a hand through his bushy hair, he started toward the winery.

"Just a minute," James called out. "I think I'll come along. Just to make sure the wine we test is what it appears to be."

A dark flush spread over Gunther's cheeks, but he accepted James's company without comment.

As they rounded the side of the house and disappeared from view, Diana turned to Lisa in agitation. "You do see what he's after, don't you?" she appealed to her sister. "How can you think of marrying such a—"

"Oh, Diana!" Lisa exclaimed, laughing. "I think he's terrific." Her eyes darkened for a moment. "And it does make Gunther so deliciously angry!"

Diana hardly heard her. Her mind was busy considering the challenge James presented.

"What has he said to you about the winery? Have you talked to him about it?"

Lisa looked slightly uncomfortable, and Diana's heart sank.

"Well, yes," Lisa hedged. "I did bring it up with him. He promised that if we do marry, he'll do what's best for the winery."

"Lisa! You know what he means by that!"

Lisa took both of her sister's ice cold hands in her own and looked uncertainly into her eyes. "I told him that you wanted to go on running things. That there were certain standards that must be maintained. And he said he would take all that into account." She reached up and hugged her sister. "We don't have much choice, do we?" she whispered, holding her close. "He's more than willing to pour in all the money the place needs. So naturally he wants some say in what's done with it."

Diana pried herself from Lisa's grip. "Naturally," she said dryly, her eyes filled with sardonic humor. "Whatever James decides is best for us is what we'll do."

Lisa was laughing again. "I don't know, though. It's awfully fun to be almost engaged. But marriage?" She shook her golden curls. "One man for the rest of my life?" A delicate shrug rippled across her shoulders. "It seems like such a bore. I'm not sure I can go through with it." She smiled at her sister. "James is awfully special, but..." She raised her palms in wry uncertainty. "Maybe he'll give us the money without a wedding. What do you think?"

Diana stared at Lisa incredulously. She was so scatterbrained! How different they were. Diana felt like a woman poised on a rock in the middle of an alligator-infested river. She could stay and be eaten, or she could jump into the water and still suffer the same fate.

"Lisa!" she hissed, "if you don't love him, you're certainly not going to marry him."

"Oh, Diana!" The tinkling laugh rang out again. "You're so serious about everything. Of course I'm going to marry him. I'm crazy about him." The sound of the two men returning reached them, and she added conspiratorially, "Did you see the flames coming out of Gunther's ears when James put his arm around me? What do you think? Did it dent his complacency a little?"

Sweeter Than Wine 83

Diana turned away in despair. It was hopeless trying to get through to her sister now. But she would have to think of something, and soon.

CHAPTER
Six

"WELL, THAT ABOUT takes care of it." Diana pushed her hair back behind her ear as she bent over her ledger. The little office, set at the back of the winery building, was neat and comfortable, if a bit shabby. Framed photographs covered the walls, a pictorial history of prizes won and harvests celebrated. Diana sat at the ancient, scuffed desk while Gunther paced restlessly behind her.

"You estimate the fifteenth," she said, "and I have the pickers lined up from the fourteenth through the twentieth, just in case. Now we only have to hope that you're somewhere near accurate."

"Near accurate!" Gunther was incensed. "I have never been wrong yet. Just wait and see! The grapes will ripen exactly when I predict."

Diana raised her head to smile at him, but the smile died on her lips as she looked out past him through the window and caught sight of James striding out toward the vineyard.

"There he goes again," she complained. "He thinks he owns this place already."

They went to the window and watched disconsolately the man each feared for a different reason stride confidently between the rows of grapes.

"At least I forced him to admit just how good our wine is," Gunther boasted. "I knew he would have to admit defeat once he tasted the chardonnay 'seventy-nine and our cabernet sauvignon from five years ago."

"Oh, he admitted it all right," Diana agreed ruefully. "And he got us to lay out all our assets without an ounce of effort on his part."

"What do you mean? He was slandering our wine! Now he knows just how much potential there is."

"Yes." She sighed. "But don't you see? I'm sure he set us up for it. He made light of our wine so that we would indignantly bring out our best. Now we can't dissuade him from taking over the winery because of the inferiority of its product."

"Well," Gunther grumbled, "that would never have worked anyway. Everyone knows we're improving all the time."

Diana didn't bother to press her point. She saw very little use to it. James Stuart always seemed to be one step ahead of her.

The previous evening had become more and more strained. Gunther and James had returned with bottles of some of the best wine Kingston Winery had ever produced, and Gunther had set about to prove their superiority. As Diana watched, staying mainly in the background, Lisa and Gunther kept up a verbal sparring match, disputing everything from judgment on wine quality to dates when certain storms or early harvests or the introduction of new procedures had occurred.

Their squabbling went on and on until finally Diana realized that James was as quiet as she was, that he was concentrating on judging the quality of the wine, paying very little attention to what Lisa and Gunther were telling him. She could almost see his analytical mind working coldly, storing facts and forming opinions. He had set them up for just this display, so that he could most accurately make his appraisal.

When his eyes had met hers, there had been only the distant blue-eyed glaze of a mind preoccupied by other matters. He had forgotten that she even existed. His thoughts were all on business.

This morning she had run into him everywhere, strolling through the aging cellar, running his hand along the sides of the oak aging barrels, poking about the laboratory, looking into the record books, checking out the crushing and pressing equipment. Each time he had favored her with an abstracted smile and gone on about his snooping, disregarding her angry glares.

He was looking over the property as though he were considering investing in it. But Diana and her sister would be the ones to pay the price.

"He's going to take over, Gunther," she said softly, her hands twisting about the pencil in her fingers. "He's going to marry Lisa and take over the winery."

She waited, half hoping the German would protest what she had said, perhaps bring up some idea that would stop the Stuart invasion cold. But he said nothing. He merely stood by her side, looking out over the land as she did, his pale face reflecting his own pessimism.

"You know it too, don't you?"

Without answering the question, Gunther suddenly

exploded into a string of Germanic curses. "The man must be stopped," he insisted savagely. "He will destroy everything! He will take our grapes and blend them with soda pop." He turned toward her in anger. "We must stop him."

It was Saturday morning. Diana still had to endure the rest of the day, and all of the next day, in James's company. Suddenly the thought seemed insufferable. She had to escape, if only for a few hours.

"I am getting out of here," she told Gunther firmly. "If you see Lisa, tell her I've gone to the tennis club for the afternoon. If you see James," she went on, her eyes sparkling with bitterness, "tell him I've gone to the moon."

The drive to the club lifted her spirits. It had been months since she had taken the time to drop by and visit with old friends, and as she stepped into the brightly lit room, with its view of the courts from conveniently placed tables, she regretted having stayed away for so long.

"Diana! How good to see you!" several friends called out, and she stopped to chat with first one group and then another. Finally she paused from sharing humorous reminiscences with two old sorority sisters to spot a familiar figure at a corner table.

"Tony Jordan!" She walked up to the handsome blond. "What are you doing here?"

Tony was an old beau of Lisa's. At one time Diana had thought he might be the one to actually pin her sister down and capture her wayward heart. In fact Diana had been rooting for him, for he was her favorite of all the men Lisa had ever dated. But Tony had been no more successful than any of the others, and finally he had left to take over his family's oil operation in a tiny country in the Middle East.

"Diana." He rose to embrace her, placing a friendly

kiss on her silky cheek. "You're more beautiful than ever."

The statement embarrassed her slightly, for she always felt that comments like that, from people who knew Lisa, were said more out of compassion than conviction. But looking into his dark brown eyes, she suddenly saw that he meant it.

"Join me," he invited, helping her into a chair. "And tell me all about the Kingston family."

She did just that, and they lingered over a light luncheon salad, laughing over past incidents, reviving old memories. Diana wished once again that things had worked out between Tony and her sister. He was such a genuinely nice person, so right for Lisa.

Suddenly Tony hesitated in the middle of a sentence, and Diana, reading his expression as he gazed out past her, knew Lisa had entered the room.

His eyes said it all. He still cared. He was still overwhelmed by the beauty that she carried with her like a casual lace shawl.

In the few seconds it took for Lisa to approach their table, Diana formed a battle plan. Tony and Lisa must find each other again. Being again in Tony's company, notoriously fickle Lisa would see that he was much better suited for her than James was. Could it possibly work?

Diana spun around to look at her sister, and her heart sank when she saw that James was with her. She noticed something else too—just how stunning the two of them looked together, Lisa with her cloud of sunshine hair, in her short tennis skirt that showed off her gorgeous legs; James with his air of command, his rugged bearing, his handsome face. He was dressed in a white shirt and tennis shorts that showed off his athletic musculature to full advantage. At the sight of him, desolation swept through Diana once again. He and Lisa looked like a dream couple, the sort that stood in front of mansions in ads for expensive cars. She felt as out of place as a mule at a horse show.

But Tony hardly seemed to notice James at all. He only had eyes for Lisa.

"Darling," he breathed reverently. "Oh, Lisa."

Lisa took it as her due. "Tony! How great to see you again." She avoided his kiss, turning instead to introduce him to James.

"This is James Stuart. My almost fiancé."

"Almost fiancé?" Tony looked from one to the other with barely concealed amusement. "And what, pray tell, is an almost finacé?"

"I'm not sure," James said smoothly. "Lisa makes up the definitions as she goes along."

He turned lazily toward Diana, and he arched an eyebrow in recognition. "Hello, Diana," he said huskily. "We hoped we would run into you here."

She turned away without a reply. Why did he torture her this way? He had Lisa. With Lisa came the winery. What was the point of trying to have her too?

They all sat down together. Looking out over the tennis players darting back and forth across the green courts, Diana knew she had to do something quickly.

Her glance rounded the table again, noting how quickly Lisa and Tony had fallen back into their old familiarity, then colliding with James's crystal blue gaze. He sat next to her at the corner of the tiny table, and his mocking eyes examined her long legs, left bare by the short white skirt of her tennis outfit. She was glad that a summer outdoors in the vineyards had left her with a smooth, brown tan, but the pleasure with which he went about his slow, languorous inspection still annoyed her.

"How about a game of mixed doubles?" she suggested to them. When there was general agreement, another thought occurred to her.

"Tony and I are both such good players, maybe we ought to play opposite each other," she said speculatively. Tony had won as many men's tournaments here at the club as she herself had won in the women's division, so it gave her a good excuse to throw Tony and Lisa together on the same side. It was a moment before she realized that this device left her paired with James.

"Sounds great to me." Tony was beaming, his eyes full of Lisa's sunshine.

As they walked toward the court, James stepped in beside Diana. "Always weaving plots, aren't you princess?" His voice was low and sensual, and when he turned toward her, his mouth twisted in a slow smile. "Just be careful you don't get caught in your own web."

It felt good to be back out on the court again, running hard after the furry balls, slamming her tennis racket through the air, sliding to a stop before the net. But her lack of play in the last few years was soon apparent in her awkward movements and disappointing speed. She had forgotten that Lisa had been at the club every weekend, her game improving just as quickly as Diana's had been deteriorating. Tony was playing well also, and it soon struck her that if it weren't for James's tenacity, the two of them would have been quickly routed by the opposing team.

She missed an easy passing shot, then drove another return into the net. As everyone else played competently, she began to feel more and more inadequate. What made it all the more embarrassing was her having lumped herself with Tony as a good player. Now she was proving to be the worst of the lot. Her cheeks took on a crimson hue, and her breathing became ragged.

"I'm sorry," she blurted out to James as she missed another passing shot. She turned toward him, full of chagrin. He stopped and looked down into her face, his own showing slight surprise, puzzlement. "Are you?" he asked, then smiled as though in genuine affection, and she felt her heart lurch as she stared up into that smile. His face looked so dark as it blocked out the sun, the rays spilling out around him like a golden halo. His blue eyes blazed in that darkness, piercing her with an icy fire that set off a current of electric sparks in her veins.

"Yes, I am." She brightened, and smiled back at him. "And I'm going to do better now."

She was as good as her word. Dashing around at top speed, diving for low shots and jumping for the high, she gave it all she had. Little by little their score crept up until finally it was within range of their opponents'.

"Deuce," Tony called out, and promptly served an ace that sped right past Diana.

"Our advantage." He grinned, and she steeled herself.

James returned the next serve well, but Tony's lob was beyond James's reach from his position at the net, and Diana had to run for it. She thought it had gone by her, but she reached for it anyway, stretching as far as she had ever stretched before, leaping through the air toward it, and feeling a quiver of delight as her racket connected with the ball, sending a solid shot whizzing right by Lisa.

As Diana made the shot, she lost her balance and crashed dizzily toward the court surface. A strong arm saved her, and she found herself being held up against James's broad chest.

"Oh!" She hung on to him, a laugh beginning to rise in her throat. As she looked up into his eyes, she saw that he was laughing too. For one golden moment their eyes met in a sudden, joyful bubble of amusement that enclosed them together, shutting out everyone else. She rested against him, feeling his rapid heartbeat and the heat of his body, and laughing into his eyes.

As the moment passed, he reached out one hand and cupped her cheek for just a few seconds, his eyes narrowing with some emotion she could not identify. Then it was over.

"It's deuce again," Tony called, preparing to send over another of his nasty first serves, and Diana went back into the play. She was inspired now. Instead of disconcerting her, the encounter with James fired her with renewed energy. When Tony's ball came spinning across the net, she sent it back with a twist that he couldn't handle.

"Good shot," James growled, and she glowed with pleasure.

From then on there was no contest. James leaped for impossible shots like a muscular gazelle, and Diana seemed to have more arms than an octopus. No place on the court was too far for one of them to reach, no ball too high or too fast. They won, and when the last ball was called out, they turned to each other in triumph.

"A victory kiss," James murmured, and then she was in his strong arms, soaring through space with the energy his mouth transmitted. They were both laughing again as his lips ceased their pressure, laughing for the pure pleasure of it all.

She wanted it to go on forever. For a brief moment her joy was complete. Nothing else mattered. She wanted to reach out and pull James to her, to bury her face in his chest and never look out into the real world again. Oh God, a part of her cried out in anguish even in the middle of her happiness. Why did she have to love him so?

She pulled away guiltily, shooting a look at the others to see what they thought of her strange behavior. But they were laughing over their own mistakes, teasingly chastising one another for missed chances, and hadn't noticed Diana and James.

Diana held her racket tightly and began to walk mechanically back to the clubhouse. Something had changed.

She could never go back again. It was out in the open now. She loved him. And he must know it too.

He was beside her again. She felt him before she saw him. Her eyes swept up his figure in a long, slow appraisal. "You'd better stay with Lisa," she hissed, but he pulled her to a stop with a strong hand on her arm.

"I warned you about getting caught in your own web," he said, his voice so low that it rumbled against her. "You can try to hide it all you want, Diana, but the carefully maintained cover is beginning to crack."

She tried to pull away, looking back toward the court where Lisa and Tony were still arguing playfully, but instead of letting her go, he forced her closer.

"That mellow silver is in your hair again," he murmured softly. "It looks like a crown for a princess." He smiled knowingly into her eyes. "Oh, princess, how am I going to slay a dragon for you when you won't even let me in?"

Diana closed her eyes and sighed. "James, will you please not talk nonsense? Sometimes I think you and I don't speak the same language at all. The things you say make no sense."

His smile expressed his exasperation. "Diana, it would make sense if you would only listen. You're the one who refuses to hear the words. I'm going to have to find another way to get through to you."

His fingers were making lazy patterns on her arm. "What shall it be, my princess? Give me a clue to the secret password."

The sound of voices from behind them indicated the approach of Tony and Lisa, and James reluctantly loosened his grip on Diana's arm. But his eyes still burned down into hers, intense with resolution.

"The winners have to stand the losers to a lemonade," Lisa called to them. "It's only fair after bruising our egos so severely."

Diana and James turned to greet the losing pair, and Diana was vividly aware of the hand still on her arm. Tony's eyes sharpened as he noticed it too, and he shot a quiet look at James. Lisa seemed serenely unperturbed.

"What are you two so deep in discussion over?" she asked airily. "You look more like losers than we do!"

"We were just trying to decide where to go tonight," Diana thrust in smoothly, ignoring James's questioning glance. "We decided on Grisson's. Will you join us, Tony? We'd love to have you."

He agreed suavely to the invitation, and Diana thought she detected a speculative look in his eyes as he glanced at James. She hoped he was judging his chances of moving in on Lisa. If so, he would be following her plans exactly.

"So you two are almost engaged," Tony said with studied casualness when they were all seated again at their table. "When is the happy event almost going to take place?"

"Oh, heavens!" Lisa trilled, her laughter bubbling out to include them all. "We've only just become almost engaged. One step at a time!"

"I hope you mean to take good care of Lisa," Tony said lightly, his eyes on James and a slight frown furling his brow. An undertone in his voice signaled a wary challenge. "Some of us around here think pretty highly of her. We wouldn't like it if anything went wrong."

James slowly raised his head, his eyes glinting with wry amusement. He stared at Tony for one long minute before saying, "There won't be a problem, Jordan." His voice was so soft that Diana wasn't sure if he meant the words to be threatening or reassuring. "I'll always make sure she's treated just as a Kingston deserves to be treated."

Diana turned a questioning glance toward him, wondering what he was trying to say, but his slow wink only confused her more. She looked away. Why did he always seem to be playing games with them all?

Lisa began fussing over Tony, apparently flattered by his concern and letting him know it. A quick glance at the others told Diana she could talk to James for a moment without being overheard. She turned to look into his eyes, wishing she could read his thoughts.

"Are you ever going to fill me in on the rules of this game?" she asked sharply. "Or is torture one of your latest hobbies?"

His gaze caressed her lips, so near as she spoke, and his breath swept across her cheek in a warm breeze that was as seductive as a siren's song. When she got this close to him, she felt she was under an enchanted spell. She found it difficult to move, to keep control over her own thoughts and actions. Time seemed to slip out of joint, and she was back again in the warm circle of his love. All she wanted was to curl up in his arms, to feel his heart beating in harmony with her own. Everything else around them seemed to fade into the background. She swayed even closer, hypnotized by the veiled mystery in his eyes.

"Diana!"

She jerked back with a start that sent color flooding her face. Looking up, she caught Tony's frown, but Lisa still seemed oblivious to the current of tension running among them.

Lisa said something innocuous, asking for her agreement on some irrelevant opinion, and Diana smiled, pretending to be taking it all in, but not hearing a word. She felt an overpowering need to get away from James, from his hold on her. The waitress hadn't yet been by to take their order, and she used that as an excuse.

"I'm so thirsty," she murmured when there was a break in the conversation. "I think I'll just pop over to the bar and order our lemonades there."

Sweeter Than Wine

She rose so quickly that she nearly overturned her chair and fled from the table without looking at any of them, threading her way through the crowded room, her eyes fixed singlemindedly on the bar. It wasn't until she reached it that she realized James had come with her.

"Oh no," she groaned when her eyes met his. "Don't you understand that you're the reason I had to leave the table?"

"Of course I know it," he growled harshly into her ear as he pressed up beside her at the counter. "That's precisely why I followed you." A hand on her arm stopped her instinctive turn to flee, and he swore softly. "I'm sorry," he said shortly. "I didn't mean that. Somehow you seem to bring out the worst side of me."

She stood stiffly, avoiding his eyes.

"I came to help you get the drinks," he continued, though he made no further move toward the bartender. "But I want to ask you something first."

She turned her head back toward him, looked up into his eyes, and waited. There was a din about them, a constant hubbub of noise and movement, but it had all faded from her consciousness. They might have been alone on a windswept plateau.

"What happened with Lawrence?" he asked softly, his eyes probing hers. "Why didn't you go ahead and marry him?"

She shook her head slowly. A sudden resentment ignited her anger. "I never wanted to marry him. How often do I have to say that?" She felt her cheeks blaze. "But I've got a question for you. Why didn't you go ahead and marry me?"

His startled eyes raked over her. "Marry you? It was made quite clear to me that I would never be good enough. Marriage to my brand of vermin would have tarnished the Kingston name."

"James..." She had no idea what he was talking

about. Something in their separate memories of the past didn't fit together. It was as if they had each lived different scenes. Perhaps if she could get it all straightened out, she'd have an answer to her unresolved confusion.

"What are you holding against me?" she asked fiercely, catching hold of his arm. "Tell me why you keep saying these things."

For some reason her words made him angry. "Saying what things?" he asked coldly. "The truth? What's wrong, Diana, can't you face the truth? Don't you like remembering how it really was?"

She wasn't getting through to him. She didn't understand his cryptic comments. Her head was in a whirl from the heady sense of his presence, from the love and resentment he stirred in her.

Taking her hand from his arm, she spun on her heel and hurried out of the building and across the blacktop toward her car.

CHAPTER
Seven

DIANA'S HEAD WAS aching as she sped across the rolling hills, pushing the Triumph much too fast along the two-lane highway. She passed vineyard after vineyard, some with barnlike wineries, some with modern steel-and-glass facilities. Her favorites were the old ones, the natural stone or Spanish-style adobe structures that she knew had been there since the turn of the century. But today she roared by them all without a second glance.

What a mess she was in. She was about to lose her winery and the man she loved, all in one fell swoop.

The man she loved. She could face it now. But just how far would her love take her? Would she want him if he indicated that he wanted her? Could she take him, knowing that he was really after her winery?

Never. Kingston pride made her raise her chin high, and she said the word out loud. "Never!"

She skidded to a stop before her vine-covered home, then groaned as she saw Gunther walking toward her from his apartment. She didn't want to talk to him now. She needed time to think.

"Are the others coming too?" he called out as he strode up to her car. When she shook her head wearily, he nodded in satisfaction. "Good. I've made a decision. Come on, let's discuss it."

He helped her out of the car, taking her arm as they went into the house. "Well, tell me," she urged, not feeling particularly hopeful that Gunther might have had a stroke of genius.

He nodded, but didn't speak until they were in the study, standing in the streaming afternoon sunlight. His eyes had a wild look as he gazed out over the land. "Lisa can't marry James," he said, his voice tense.

Diana smiled at his fierce grimace. "I agree entirely. But what are we going to do about it?"

He looked down at the ground and ran his hand distractedly through his fawn-colored hair, his cheeks suddenly stained red from his discomfort. "I will marry her myself," he said softly.

Diana looked at him intently, not sure that she had heard correctly. "What was that?"

Suddenly he was glaring at her defiantly. "I will marry her myself," he proclaimed proudly. "Then we will see no more of this James Stuart."

He wasn't joking. All at once she saw that what she had taken for a harmless crush had turned into something more. But there was something incongruous in the thought of Lisa with Gunther. He was nothing like the men Lisa usually went out with.

Sweeter Than Wine

A feeling of pity welled up in her. How could she explain it wouldn't work without hurting his feelings? She gazed at him helplessly, wishing she could think of something to say.

And as she looked at him, his face so clear and determined, she realized what a good friend he had been all these years, and how much affection she felt for him. For all his stodgy, opinionated ways, he was a true and loyal partner. She hated to see him hurt.

"Gunther, I don't know what to say."

"You don't think I have a chance, do you?"

He had hit the truth on the first try, but how could she admit it? She wet her lips with the tip of her tongue, looking about the room for support. "I don't have the slightest idea what kind of chance you have," she hedged. "Lisa has always been an enigma to me." A sudden thought occurred to her. "But I don't know if you've given yourself a chance." She looked him straight in the eye. "Have you told her how you feel?"

He looked uncomfortable. "No. I have great difficulty in expressing these things. I want you to tell her."

Diana's jaw dropped in astonishment. "Me?" she squeaked. "Are you crazy?"

"Why not?" he said in defense of the idea. "She's your sister. You can tell her how I feel. Tell her I wish to marry her. We will see what she says."

Diana suppressed a smile. "How do *you* feel, Gunther? You haven't really said."

He frowned. "I think I've made it clear enough."

She shook her head. "No, you haven't. Say the words."

"I won't. There is no need..."

But she wouldn't let him get away with that. Standing before him with her hands on her hips, she insisted, "Say it."

He avoided her eyes and said very softly, "I love her."

Diana smiled warmly. "There. That wasn't all that difficult. Now that you've said it to me, you can say it to her."

A look of absolute panic clouded his eyes. "Diana, I can't!"

She inclined her head sternly. "But you must." Reaching up, she gave his disheveled hair a friendly tousle. "Think it over. You can do it. And you'll never win her if you don't."

Looking around the room, she picked up a sweater from the back of her desk chair. "I'm going to run over and see Millie. Maybe, they'll be gone when I get back."

She left Gunther standing in the study staring after her and hurried back to her car. She really did want to get away before the others got back. It might be just as well to try to keep away from James from now on. He had two rivals actively hoping to thwart his plans. She might just as well stand back and let Gunther and Tony try their hand at it.

"Come on in and give me a hand with this salad!"

Millie's cheerful voice rang out even before Diana stepped out of her car. She walked into the little cottage with a smile, already sensing Millie's good mood.

"I'm trying to use up the rest of these late tomatoes," Millie said. "Aren't they beauties? I put in Better Boys this year, and they're much juicier than the variety I planted last summer. And I didn't get nearly as many tomato worms."

With a friendly grin, she handed Diana a paring knife and a finger-sized zucchini. "Slice this up while I check to see if there are any cucumbers left. I used up the last of the regular ones, but I think there might be an Armenian still on the vine."

She disappeared while Diana did as she'd been told.

Millie was back in minutes carrying one of the long, curved green vegetables that were her special pride. "Look at this! Almost two feet long," she said proudly as she entered the kitchen. As Diana admired Millie's Armenian cucumber, she thought she detected a new gleam in her friend's eyes.

"You look chipper," she said approvingly. "What have you been up to since I saw you last?"

Millie gave her a sidelong glance. "I'll tell you all about it when we sit down to eat," she said smugly, as though holding back a great secret.

"All right," Diana agreed. "I guess that means I'm going to get a free meal."

"Of course you are. That is, as long as you'll be satisfied with my simple fare."

She sprinkled Italian dressing on the salad. "There's iced tea in the refrigerator and fresh sourdough bread in the basket. Help me carry it all outside to the picnic table, and the feast will begin."

The picnic table stood under two massive oak trees and boasted a view of the vineyards that had once belonged to Millie and her husband. The rows of vines were bordered by golden fields of hay.

"Stunning, isn't it?" Millie said, nodding toward the grapevines. Some varieties were already turning apple red or tarnished gold in the cool autumn air. "At least I have this sight to sustain me." She changed the topic of conversation. "I called your friend," she said happily.

Diana was pleased. "Beth Wheeler? I'm so glad. I'm sure you'll become close."

"We're already on the road to that. I stopped by on Thursday to meet her for lunch, and when we finished eating, I found myself corraled into attending a meeting with her." She chuckled, her face all smiles. "And you know me. At that meeting, I just couldn't help but raise my hand when they asked for volunteers. So now I'm on the housing committee, and we're picketing a landlord on Monday."

"Wait a minute," Diana said, laughing. "One thing at a time. What was the meeting all about? And why are you picketing?"

Millie waved away the details. "The meeting was a forum for senior citizens with problems that might apply to other people as well. And the housing committee is actively involved in trying to get landlords to stop converting their apartments to condominiums, thereby forcing many people out of their homes because they can no longer afford them."

"And is that what this picketing is all about?"

Millie shook her gray head. "Not exactly. This case is even worse. The landlord is tearing down perfectly good apartments and turning the whole site into a parking garage."

Diana had a sudden intuition. "What's the name of this building?" she asked quietly.

"The Nordon Building," Millie answered. "It's owned by some big corporation whose executives think they can put cars over people."

Diana bit her lower lip. "Don't you know the name of that corporation?" she asked.

Millie squinted, then shook her head. "I don't think I ever caught that. We're meeting down at Union Square."

"Millie," Diana said warningly. "That building belongs to Stuart Enterprises. You're going to be picketing James Stuart himself."

Sudden silence trembled between them. "Oh!" Millie said finally in a small voice. "Oh gosh!"

Diana laughed at the anguished expression on her

friend's face. "Now don't let that influence you. If it's wrong, it's wrong. The identity of the landlord shouldn't make any difference."

"I suppose you're right."

It took a few minutes to restore the glow of excitement to Millie's cheeks, but before Diana left, she managed it. And as she drove back toward home, she felt better herself. Millie's company was always uplifting.

Gunther was waiting for her at the house when she returned.

"They've all gone to Grisson's," he announced glumly. "We're all alone."

"Why didn't you go with them?"

He shrugged unhappily. "I tried to talk to Lisa, but James was always hanging about, and then Tony arrived." He cast Diana a gloomy look. "So I decided not to go."

Diana shook her head. "We're a fine pair," she said softly. Sudden determination filled her. "A fine pair of losers. This won't do." Turning toward Gunther, she began propelling him toward the door.

"Go back to your place and get all dressed up. We're both going to stop this hanging back. It's time we took matters in hand."

She could see he was about to protest, but one look at her resolute expression seemed to quell it. She closed the door behind him and hurried up the stairs.

Looking into her closet, she despaired. Everything seemed frumpy, and she knew that Lisa would be stunning. Without considering her motives or the consequences of her action, she dashed across the hall to her sister's room, threw open the doors of her closet, and pulled out a large number of dresses. She chose one she thought would be flattering and hurried back to her own room, where she took a quick shower and fixed her hair. Lightly applied makeup added shine to her complexion and a shimmer to her lips, and she was ready to go.

Gunther stared at her as she walked down the stairs, but she was satisfied with the shocked admiration in his eyes. She knew that the dress she had chosen was daring, but she didn't care.

She had piled her black hair on top of her head, leaving curled wisps dangling along her neckline. She wore a bright scarlet halter dress, fitted through the waist and hips with a swirling transparent gauze skirt that clung to her shapely legs. The gossamer fabric cupped her breasts, barely concealing their peaks, then clasped behind her neck, leaving a significant portion of bare skin.

"Do you like it?" she asked Gunther, but he was too stunned to reply and quickly threw her black lace shawl about her shoulders, as though attempting to shield her from the world's examination. She sensed the protest trembling on his lips, but he seemed too embarrassed to put it into words, and she laughed.

"No one said a word when Lisa wore this to the Hunters' Ball last spring," she announced defiantly. "And I want to wear it too."

Much to Diana's surprise, Gunther himself looked fine. He had found a white dinner jacket, and a hint of Diana's new fire seemed to have rubbed off on him. She cocked her head and looked at the man again, smiling softly as she noted that he wasn't bad looking when his hair was combed flat.

They rode to the supper club in silence. Diana was grateful that for once Gunther's tongue was stilled. She didn't want to see James, yet she longed to. She hoped he wouldn't be there, that for some reason he and Lisa might have gone on to some other entertainment. Yet she knew she would be disappointed if they had.

Sweeter Than Wine

Grisson's was one of the favorite weekend night spots in the valley. A live band played mostly old standards, and couples danced the evening away under the stars on a lovely open terrace surrounded by a camellia tree garden that sheltered innumerable private walkways.

Raising her head in proud, daring rebellion, Diana swept in before Gunther like a queen among her subjects. They made their way through the crowded restaurant and continued on to a group of tables that ringed the opening to the terrace. James was the first to see her. When their eyes met, she saw nothing else. As she slowly approached, his gaze never left hers. His eyes looked huge and black in the darkened room, his face as still and impassive as that of an old world lord. He didn't smile. He made no sign that he welcomed her, and she felt chilled by his cold reception, but excited at the same time. She could feel his glance rake over her, taking in every curve, every inch of her exposed skin, and she resisted the impulse to pull her shawl more tightly around her shoulders.

A voice deep inside cried a warning, questioning her sanity, but she stilled it. This was something she had to do, though she didn't know why.

"Diana!"

Lisa and Tony had seen her now too, and they turned in their seats to gape at the picture she made, a bright, crimson flame of light flickering nearer in the gloomy room.

"Hello, everybody."

James rose and helped her into the booth between him and Tony, facing Lisa and Gunther. Though her heart was pounding, Diana kept a smile on her face, hoping no one would notice how her hands were shaking.

None of the others said a word, but it seemed to Diana that their emotions were written on their faces. Gunther was defiant, his slim jaw tight and his blue eyes ferocious. Tony was a cynical observer, watching it all with reserved amusement. Lisa was speculative, her silver-blue eyes flickering from one man to another. Every one of them was here because of Lisa, Diana realized with a sense of quiet acceptance. It had always been that way.

Why had she come? Some twisted idea in her head that she would win James back from Lisa tonight had brought her here, some farfetched thought that while Lisa was busy handling Gunther and Tony, Diana would convince James to give up all ideas of marrying Lisa. Diana could see now how silly that idea had been. As always, Lisa was the focal point of the group.

Besides, once Diana won James, what was she prepared to do with him? No, the whole idea was much too risky.

James's expression was the only one she found impossible to interpret. His eyes were still dark, mysterious pools in his granite-hard face, and his tense jaw suggested some barely leashed emotion. But she didn't know what it meant. She never could read him.

"You look lovely, Diana," Tony drawled, his knowing eyes sweeping over her.

"Yes," Lisa said, smiling warmly at her sister. She raised her eyebrows in comical distress and whispered loudly, "Just don't do anything to ruin that dress. I was planning to wear it to the Historical Society Evening next week."

Gunther assumed a look of firm resolution. "Yes, Diana is lovely, isn't she?" he proclaimed loudly, smiling at her with the proprietary air of one who expected to soon be her brother-in-law. "It's time the rest of you realized what a jewel has been hiding under your noses." He turned to include Lisa in his blue gaze.

"Waitress," he called imperially, gesturing with his

Sweeter Than Wine   109

free hand. "The wine list, please. We must order something suitably rare and fine with which to toast the beauty of the two women accompanying us tonight."

Suddenly Tony seemed to lose his objectivity. He glared at Gunther through narrow brown eyes, as though he had suddenly identified him as a new rival. "Well, vintner," he growled, "so now you have become an expert on women as well as on wine."

Gunther laughed in an unpleasant, belligerent manner that alarmed Diana. She tried to catch his eye, hoping to calm him. "Wine, women, and song, Mr. Jordan. I try to be a connoisseur of all the finer things." With a flourish, he picked up Lisa's slim hand from where it lay on the table beside him and brought it to his lips in a courtly, old world fashion.

Lisa's pleased laugh rang across the table. Tony pulled himself up straighter in his seat with slow deliberateness, his eyes on the hand Gunther still held.

"I hope you treat your wines with a lighter touch than you do your women," Tony ground out harshly. "From my experience the grape does not appreciate a mauling, though I've heard certain women prefer it."

His eyes flashed a sharp look at Gunther, and the air seemed alive with the electricity of their sudden competition.

Diana turned to James in wonder and found him trying vainly to suppress his amusement.

"This isn't funny," she whispered. "You've got to stop them."

"Why?" His eyes were wide with innocence. "I wouldn't miss it for the world." He grinned, and she had the uncomfortable feeling that he meant far more than he said.

She turned to look at Gunther and found him glaring at Tony with ill-concealed distaste. Tony, for his part, was staring back with the look of a man who was about to accept a challenge.

"The music is marvelous," she said quickly. "Why don't we all dance?"

"Fine," Tony said bluntly. "I'll dance with Lisa, you take Gunther."

"No," James interposed smoothly. "Diana has promised this dance to me."

They left the two other men glaring at each other, with Lisa sitting serenely between them. As James pulled Diana into his arms, she found herself leaning her head against his chest to hide her laughter.

"Silly, aren't they?" he agreed. "But so entertaining."

"Even for you?" She looked up in his face, wondering what he really felt.

"Why not for me?" he returned. "I have a sense of humor too."

"But..." She hesitated, wondering just how much she dared say. "You're rather directly involved."

"Am I?" He tried to pull her back close against him, but she resisted, wanting to see his reaction.

"Aren't you?" she echoed, tilting her chin and narrowing her eyes.

He stared back at her, swaying with the music, not letting her see beyond the azure veil of his eyes. "What would you do if I married Lisa?" he asked suddenly.

She winced, then lowered her eyes to cover her response. "I'd go on managing the winery, of course," she said bravely. "What would you do?"

His arm seemed suddenly harder against her back. "What if I took over at the winery?" he asked softly. "What if I used my influence and resources to merge it with my other concerns?"

She steeled herself, then forced her gaze to meet his again. "Then I'd leave," she answered with more firm-

Sweeter Than Wine 111

ness than she felt. "I might try to get a job with another winery. Maybe in the Santa Cruz area."

This time when he pulled her against him, she couldn't stop him. He held her very tightly and murmured into her hair, "No. I don't want you to leave."

She closed her eyes, listening to his heartbeat, so close to her cheek, and thought, Then don't take over my winery. But she couldn't say it. As she swayed with him to the last strains of the melody, she couldn't say a word.

They had been the only ones dancing, and when they returned to the table, they found that a row of wine bottles had been placed from one end to the other. A wide-ranging variety of pinot noir, they were all vintage-dated and of excellent quality. Pairs of sparkling crystal glasses stood before each one.

"All right, o expert one," Tony was challenging, his eyes glowing angrily. "Let's see how well the connoisseur ranks in wine tasting. Let's see your genius in action."

Gunther's eyes gleamed with delight. He was in his element. Diana slid back into the seat, looking at Tony with curious concern. She was just a little bit afraid that he had already had more to drink than he should.

Lisa was smiling benignly on them all, as though she were used to enticing such silly behavior. On either side of her, Tony and Gunther both seemed bent on making fools of themselves.

Diana looked to James for help, but he merely grinned at her and leaned back in his seat. "This is better than a comedy act," he murmured, but only Diana seemed to hear.

Tony took the first sample, swirling the wine in the glass, heating it with the warmth of his palm, then sniffing the bouquet before letting a splash flow across his tongue.

"Rich," he proclaimed. "Full-bodied, but a bit young. It needs more time." He looked at the label on the bottle. "Ah yes. That was the year of the late frost. It added a certain mellow richness, as I am sure you will see for yourself."

Gunther went through the same procedure, but shook his head. "Decent but dull," he announced. "Your taste is mundane, Mr. Jordan."

A flush of outrage appeared on Tony's usually mild face. He reached for the next wine.

"The garnet red color is good. Aroma soft; bouquet with a hint of oak. The taste is complex, with fine balance. But I would judge it less than exquisite."

"Wrong again," Gunther declared. "This is an absolutely stylish wine. You don't have the finely tuned taste necessary to recognize its attributes." Ignoring the snort of fury from across the table, he took another taste and savored it. "This is a jewel of a wine. It has the irresistible, silky body of..." He hesitated, and his eyes, which had been roaming about the assembly, stopped at Lisa. "... the silky body of an elegant woman," he concluded, lowering his voice, the throb in it leaving no one in doubt as to whose body he was referring to.

Diana watched Lisa's pleasure in the compliment and uttered a silent bravo for Gunther.

But Tony didn't see it quite that way. "What a farce," he said. "You ignorant lout. If you know no more about woman than you do about wines—"

"I know more about Lisa than you ever will." The outburst had been an infuriated ejaculation, but Gunther regained control before he finished it. Temper again in leash, he ground out, "The next wine, maestro," and poured for them both.

Diana felt slightly perplexed. This had to be the most ridiculous exhibition she had ever witnessed. They were using the excuse of wine tasting to insult one another.

She looked at James and mouthed, "I don't believe this!"

He grinned, winked, and leaned forward to pour a pair of taste samples.

Handing one to Diana, he sniffed loudly into the bowl of his glass, took a gross swallow, and intoned solemnly, with a thickly artificial British slur, "It has a rather loud shout, don't you think? But behind all the bravado lurks a coward of a grape."

Diana concealed a grin behind her own sip as she joined him. "Absolutely," she agreed in the most supercilious voice she could adopt. "The kiss excites, but when one probes more deeply, it merely teases."

The other two men gazed at them with ill-concealed impatience, but they weren't about to give up the floor.

"Try this one, Diana." James poured her a glass from the next bottle. "I would like your considered opinion."

She shook her head sadly after tasting it. "It rather misses the point, don't you think? But one must appreciate how hard it tries."

"Yes," he agreed. "She's a round, full-bodied little flirt, but she turns flabby in the end."

With her nose in the air, but her laughter just barely held back, Diana met the smiling gaze James shot her. Their eyes held as she pronounced, "Now here is a wine that is as exciting as a rake, and just as quick to vanish once he's had his way."

There was a moment of tense silence, then Lisa exploded into a burst of laughter, the sound pealing through the room. Gunther and Tony beside her had the good grace to attempt smiles.

"Let's get out of here," James whispered in Diana's ear, "before they start in again. I don't think I have any more phony pronouncements left in my repertoire."

He stood up and held out a hand to her, inviting her to dance. How could she refuse? As she rose to meet him, her heart began to beat a wild pattern in her chest, pounding blood to crimson her cheeks, to sharpen her nerves, to keep her from missing the tiniest sensation of his touch.

As he curled her into his arms, she knew she was lost. Without a token of resistance, she closed her eyes and laid her head against his broad chest. She heard no music, felt nothing but the wild joy of his closeness. It was a piece of heaven, and more than she had hoped to have.

She floated against him. The cloth between them seemed to disappear, for all she felt was the solid weight of his flesh upon her own. She felt his face in her hair, his breath stirring the tendrils, and she sighed with longing for what could never be.

"Tired?" he whispered, but she didn't answer. She didn't want to open her eyes and look up at him, for that would break the spell. For then she would have to draw away again, to freeze her feelings for her own protection.

But now she could drift, as secure in his arms as she had once been in his love.

The dance ended, and she left him with regret. Events had taken a calmer turn at the table, with Tony finally regaining his usual amused reserve.

"I don't know what came over me," he admitted as he led Diana around the floor to a snappy foxtrot. "I guess I was feeling a bit possessive of Lisa."

Diana smiled, glad to have the old Tony back again. "You were certainly going at one another there for a while," she agreed. "I was afraid we'd have to put you at separate tables."

He grinned ruefully. "Lisa seems to bring out the dog in the manger in all of us," he admitted. His dark eyes sharpened and he looked down at her again. "By the way," he went on. "It's none of my business, but I must admit to being very curious."

"Oh?" Diana had no idea what he was talking about.

Sweeter Than Wine

"What exactly is it between you and James?" he asked softly as he swept her across the floor. "And why, if he's so totally nuts over you, does he plan to marry Lisa?"

Diana stared at him, shocked. "Nuts over me? Oh no, Tony. That's one observation that's far off base."

His smile was gently chiding. "Come on, Diana. I saw what happened on the tennis court this afternoon. I saw how restless he was before you arrived, how stunned he was when he saw you in this—" he drew back to get another look at her—"this admittedly stunning dress. He's head over heels, darling. But why is he marrying Lisa?"

She shook her head, smiling sadly. How could she explain to Tony that what he read as infatuation was actually a compulsion for revenge? "Why do you think a man might want to marry Lisa? Isn't it obvious?"

"Actually, no," he answered enigmatically, but before she could question that strange statement, he went on. "And he wants you so very badly. You and he knew each other sometime in the past, didn't you?"

"Yes," she admitted. Suddenly she recalled something. Tony had been a friend of hers for years, had been to school with her. "Don't you remember?" she asked softly, searching his eyes. "The party I gave the year before we all went away to college? The one where I was going to introduce everyone to the boy I was planning to marry?"

Ordinarily she would have gone to great pains to keep anyone from remembering the incident, but Tony was different. He had always understood.

"My God!" he breathed. "Of course! I knew I'd seen him somewhere before." He looked sharply down into her face. "But he showed up with that girl and threw your love back in your face. It was the talk of the valley."

Diana nodded miserably.

"And now he's back." Tony tilted her chin up so that

he could see her eyes. "He's back and pretending to court Lisa, who is pretending that she gives a damn. It's all very confusing, my dear."

"There's more to it. Oh, Tony! It's all so awful."

"I wish I could help." His smile was bemused. "But interfering usually makes things worse. I have a feeling that they'll be sorted out in time."

But time was getting short. Diana sighed and shook her head. She wished she had Tony's optimism.

Silence held between them, and Tony said no more about it. Finally, just before the dance ended, Diana spoke again. "Do you still love Lisa, Tony?" She looked up thoughtfully into his brown eyes.

His grin was uneven. "I'll always love Lisa. She's a part of me."

"Well—" Diana almost shook him in her impatience—"do something about it. Who knows? You may get her to listen this time."

He laughed. "Oh poor Diana, if that is your only hope. Lisa and I will never get married."

"Why not?"

"I love Lisa, darling, but I also love a lot of other women. That's just the sort of person I am."

"But that's the sort of person she is too! You're perfectly suited."

Tony hugged her close and laughed again. "You'll have to find another way out of this, darling. Somehow I don't think a match between two rovers would have a great prognosis for success."

The music ended, and he walked with her back to the table, where the only face she really saw was James's.

CHAPTER
Eight

THE REST OF the evening spun by in a hazy state of unreality that Diana didn't try to penetrate. The earlier bitterness between Tony and Gunther seemed to have dissipated, and the five of them got on well for a change. A scattering of friends dropped by to chat. Most of them noticed Lisa first, but stayed to compliment Diana and bring up memories of old times with Tony.

The music was seductive, and Diana danced with every one of the men at least once. But each time James put his arms around her, she knew that was where she most wanted to be. And toward the end she danced with no one else.

The crowd had thinned, and the music had taken a melancholy turn.

"This could be the last dance of the night," James

murmured as his hand molded Diana's back. "We should do something to make it memorable."

"What did you have in mind?" she asked, feeling sleepy as they moved slowly across the dance floor.

His mouth was very near her ear. "We could always run away in the middle of it," he suggested hopefully.

She twisted to look up into his blue eyes. "We could never run away from ourselves," she said sadly.

A frown appeared on his handsome face, and though he didn't answer, he began leading their steps in lazy circles out onto the terrace. Soon they were among the camellia bushes, where the light was murky and the sound of the music came faint and far away.

They were still swaying to the music, but merely as an excuse to keep their arms around each other. Diana didn't protest. She knew how cold it was going to be when he finally let her go.

"What made you say that?" he asked evenly.

"Say what?" She drew her head back to see his expression.

"That we couldn't run away from ourselves."

She shrugged and slowly began to pull away from him. "It's true, isn't it?"

She turned and reached for a waxy camellia leaf, running her finger along its smooth edge. His hand slid silkily to the nape of her neck, and she let it stay there.

"What do you think, Diana?" he said huskily. "Is there any way to escape destiny? Does the past rule us forever?"

Yes, she thought, wishing she could deny it. She turned toward him curiously. "Do you feel that it rules you?"

He wasn't looking at her any longer. His eyes seemed to be seeing something out beyond the trees. "Sometimes it seems to."

His hand tightened on her neck. "I told you about my mother. About how the Stuarts didn't think she was good enough for my father." A muscle in his jaw had begun to twitch, as though he were clenching it too hard. "But I didn't tell you the rest. The disapproval didn't blow over once they were married. My father's family never forgave them. My grandmother and my aunts and uncles and cousins all hated my mother's background, hated her gentleness, her grammar, her dark beauty. They made her life hell, and my father did nothing to stop them. He let them make her feel she wasn't right. He wrapped himself up in his work and let them torture her until she finally gave up and ran away."

He looked down at Diana with a crooked smile. "She disappeared when I was twelve. I didn't see her again until I was twenty-four. They made sure I couldn't find her. But they didn't let me forget her." He laughed shortly. "No, her spirit was always there. Mostly as a ghost to haunt me. Every time I did anything that didn't conform to the Stuart code, anything from staying out too late to getting into trouble at school, they all looked at me and shook their heads sadly. 'Bad blood will tell,' they would mutter among themselves." He grinned again. "Sounds funny now, doesn't it? But it wasn't funny then."

The pain and anger were still raw in him, and she wished she had the right to reach out to him in comfort. Instead, she clasped her hands together, squeezing hard, and didn't utter a word of sympathy.

"Is that why you took your mother's name that summer?" she asked instead.

He nodded. "When I found my mother, I turned my back on the Stuarts. I called myself Morel and forgot all about my Ivy League background. I was going to be a man of the people."

"And that was when you worked in my father's fields."

His hand came up into her hair, turning her face toward his.

"Do you see?" he asked, suddenly filled with tension. "Can you understand why I reacted as I did that summer? Why I had to strike back?"

She searched the clouded blue eyes. What was he talking about? What had this agony over his mother to do with their love? What did it have to do with his turning away from her? Was he trying to tell her that what they had shared had somehow been in reaction to what he had experienced with his family? That she mustn't take it seriously?

She shook her head. "No, James, I don't understand," she said softly. "And I can't forget it happened or wish it away."

He touched her lips with his finger. "Maybe you're right," he murmured, groaning deep in his chest. "I thought I could see you again and walk away," he whispered fiercely. "But I can't. I won't."

He gathered her fiercely to him and began to rain kisses on her face. She felt a languorous spell taking over her body. It was as though a secret potion were mixed with the scent of flowers. Every movement she made was slowed by the heavy mist she moved in. Her usual defenses crumbled.

His hands were on her shoulders, his fingers pressing. Her arms slid around his neck, and she reached for his kiss with lips that were hungry to taste his love.

He wasted no time in asserting his possession, his tongue exploring every warm, hidden secret, slowly, sensuously caressing her as his ardor mounted. Desire sparked between them and caught fire, but James kept it under tense control, and for a moment Diana sensed sincere feeling rather than passion behind his kiss. Could it be affection?

She was glad he felt something for her. He might not love her with the wild, innocent passion they had once shared, but there was something between them. If only she could nurture that little flame and coax it back into a consuming fire.

James's hands slid down her back, cupping her hips and pulling her in against the length of his long body. It was time to retreat. She knew that, but she couldn't convince herself to act on it. Not yet.

His mouth left hers and made its way in warm, silky movements along her neck, and she tilted back her head, closing her eyes and letting the sensation spin her away into another world.

"Diana, Diana," he breathed into the pulse that throbbed at the base of her neck. "I've waited so long for this. Tell me that the wait is over."

Her hands were running through his thick rich hair, pulling his face against her skin, and she only sighed in answer, lowering her face to breathe in the illusive male aroma that perfumed his hair.

Then he raised his face to hers again, and his fingers were thrusting into her hair, pulling it from the pins that held it, holding her face before him like a valued treasure.

"Diana," he said fiercely, his eyes burning like blue flames. "You do still love me. *Say* you love me."

She tried to avoid his eyes, tried to pull away, but he was holding her much too strongly. "Let me go, James," she forced out. "I can't... you mustn't..."

But he took advantage of her parted lips to renew his seductive assault, and she found she couldn't resist his persuasion. The warmth of his deep kiss spread like molten fire through her chest. His hands made exciting patterns on her bare skin that sent electricity coursing through her body. He tantalized her about the waist and along her sides and finally just barely touched her breasts. The nipples hardened immediately against the crisp, translucent cloth of her dress.

"Oh," she gasped, pulling reluctantly away. "Stop, James, or we'll both regret it."

"Regret it?" he scoffed harshly. "Never!" He let her withdraw but still stood near enough to keep her in his spell.

"You would certainly regret it if it destroyed your almost engagement to Lisa," she said, unable to hide her bitterness.

His long fingers curled about her chin, raising her eyes to his. "The almost engagement is over," he said lightly, his eyes shining with humor.

She frowned. "Over? You mean... does Lisa know this?"

He nodded. "We had a long talk this afternoon while you were visiting Millie. Lisa and I are just good friends."

This was it, what she had prayed for. So why didn't she feel like celebrating? What was the terrible dread that constricted her breathing?

James's fingers casually brushed against her cheek, pushing back wayward tendrils of hair. "The engagement was a sham anyway," he admitted absently. "She and I each had our own silly reasons for playing with the idea. I think we both knew all along that we would never go through with it."

Diana again avoided his eyes, and wet her lips with the tip of her tongue. "I think I understand Lisa's reasons," she said shakily. "For her it was just another lark. But what were your reasons, James?"

She was pretty sure she knew, but she wanted to hear him say it, wanted to make him admit the truth and bring it out into the open between them.

His hands made a gentle collar around one side of her neck. "Don't you know, Diana?" he asked huskily. "Don't you understand yet how much I wanted revenge?"

"But why?" she cried. "What did I ever do to turn you from my lover into my worst enemy?"

His eyes glinted with annoyance. "We've been over

that enough already," he said dismissively. "I can try to forget it if you can."

She stared at him. Could she? She didn't think so.

A smile curled his wide mouth again. "Lisa thinks we're right for each other," he teased. "I think so too."

He dropped a quick, affectionate kiss on her cheek, but still she stood staring at him. What did he want from her? Love? Sex? Or her winery? She still wasn't sure.

"Lisa approves, does she?" Diana said softly. "What else did she say?"

"Once she had heard some of the background of our relationship, she told me I had picked the wrong sister this time," he said. "She told me to do what I would if I'd picked the wrong firm for a business merger—to buy out of my bad deal and try to repair the damage."

Diana's hands felt very cold. A bad business deal— was that what his relationship with Lisa had been? And was he now repairing the damage so as to pave the way for something more lucrative?

Sure Lisa was the wrong sister. She wasn't the one who ran the winery. Diana was.

"You asked me this afternoon why I never married you," he said in a low, soft voice, "and you were right. I should have." He dropped another quick kiss on her unresponsive lips. "Let's make up for that now, Diana."

He wanted to marry her. That was what he was saying. With all her heart, she wished she could feel some joy in his proposal. He was promising to make up for the past. But couldn't he see how impossible that was?

The love they had once shared had been clean and beautiful. This love he was promising was tarnished and suspect. He wanted her. She was sure of that. But he wanted her winery more.

She had been here all these long years. He could have come back any time. Why had he waited until he'd decided to become a major vintner? Why had he waited until he needed her land?

He had found it easy enough to turn away from her that summer, once he had taken all he wanted from her. What was to keep him from turning from her again?

No. She wouldn't marry him. Never.

"Give me a chance to take this all in," she told him, evading his questioning eyes. "I think we should get back to the others, don't you?"

She knew he could sense her reserve, and that he didn't like it. But as he walked at her side, he seemed to be holding in his resentment, biding his time.

With relief she found that the others were ready to call it a night. And when she was given a choice of campanions for the return trip, she quickly chose Gunther. She had endured all she could of James's company for one night.

The next morning seemed to come much too quickly. Diana wasn't able to sleep for more than intermittent snatches before the sun purpled the eastern sky. All hope of rest fled. Slipping into a sweater and slacks, she made her way quietly down the stairs and out into the garden. For a time she wandered among the rose bushes, noting how they needed pruning, and out among the trees of the fruit orchard, some hanging heavy with golden fruit, others already shedding their yellow leaves. Finally she found herself at the carp pond and sat down beside the mossy banks.

Picking up a spike of tiny blue flowers, she shook their dried seeds to the winds, then spent the next few minutes picking their strawlike husks off her lemon yellow cotton sweater and darker yellow slacks. Anything to keep from thinking of the scene she knew was coming.

It was strange how little satisfaction she derived from

Sweeter Than Wine

knowing that James would never marry Lisa. Deep down, she had never really believed in their engagement anyway. James had started out pretending to want Lisa, but he had never made any secret of his preference for her older sister. Besides, marrying Diana was a much more direct way of taking control.

She would have to tell him they didn't have a deal. She only hoped he would take her answer like the experienced businessman he was and realize this was the end.

"Good morning."

She hadn't heard him walk up behind her, and hearing his voice made her jump. But when she twisted around to look at him, she couldn't help but smile.

He wore jeans that clung tightly to his muscular legs and a plaid shirt open at the neck. Gazing up at his face, the sun blindingly bright behind him, she could almost imagine that it was six years earlier.

"Hi." Her voice was low with morning huskiness. "You're up early."

"I couldn't sleep either," he said softly, dropping to the grass beside her.

She looked at him sharply, wondering how he knew. Did she look that bad? But his smiling gaze was slipping down to caress her neck, as though he was remembering the kisses he had bestowed there the night before.

She waited nervously for him to bring up the marriage proposal again, not relishing the confrontation in store for them. She couldn't marry him. If she had the strength of her convictions, she would tell him so now and not wait for him to bring it up. She should tell him and then get up and leave—and never see him again.

But she sat beside him watching how the early breeze ruffled his silky hair and knew she couldn't do it.

He took her hand in his and slowly separated the

fingers, looking at each one as though it were special and deserving of careful attention. "What we need," he said, "is a vacation."

"A vacation?" she echoed, startled.

He nodded slowly, searching her eyes. "We need a vacation from the past. And from the future. Will you take a vacation like that with me?"

She swallowed. It was very difficult to deny him anything when he looked at her like that. "Just what did you have in mind?"

He gathered her fingers together and carried them to his lips. "Don't look so frightened," he said softly against them, a slight smile crinkling the corners of his eyes. "What I'm thinking of is a lazy day on the coast. Just some browsing, wading in the surf, a small meal. What do you say?" When she hesitated, he leaned forward. "No past, Diana. No big decisions. Just you, a woman, and me, a man, alone for the day. Please come."

"But what about Lisa?" It was her last defense—and it fell before his persuasion.

"Lisa is spending the day in bed with a fat historical novel and a sick headache. She told me so herself."

Diana had no excuses left. Looking up at him, she knew there was nothing in the world she wanted to do more.

"It sounds like fun," she admitted. "No past, no future?"

He curled his hand around hers in a bargaining shake. "Deal," he said lightly. "Shall we go?"

The sun seemed to be spilling gold over the valley as they drove through the hills into the pastoral countryside of Sonoma County.

"How about eating breakfast in Petaluma?" James suggested.

Diana nodded happily. "That sounds fine. Would you like to stop for a tour of the Adobe State Historic Park?

The old house and fort where General Vallejo lived during Spanish days is always interesting. They've turned it into a museum now."

He frowned. "I don't know. Touring museums wasn't what I had in mind for our day. I'm a bit anxious to get out to the coast."

She smiled. "Then why don't you just drive on through Petaluma? I've got a great idea for a place we can get an unusual breakfast."

The maple trees that lined Petaluma's streets had turned brilliant shades of red and orange. The trees and the red brick houses of the little town always reminded Diana of the Midwest.

"Did you know that Petaluma once rivaled Detroit in carriage building?" she asked James with a grin. "That was before a man named Ford revolutionized that industry."

They took Red Hill Road for nine miles until they arrived at the Rouge et Noir Cheese Factory which was back among the hills near a lovely stretch of water.

"We can take a guided tour and then buy enough cheese and bread for a picnic eaten on the lawn overlooking the lake," Diana suggested.

"A picnic for breakfast?" James asked doubtfully.

"Just try it," she coaxed. "You'll be surprised."

A little over an hour later, they were on their way again, pleasantly stuffed with brie and cheddar on sourdough bread.

"You were right," James admitted. "From now on, you'll be tour director. I'm gaining a healthy respect for your ideas."

They made their way to the Point Reyes National Seashore, stopping to watch the clammers searching for gapers on Tomales Bay and the trainers working horses at the Morgan Horse Farm in Bear Valley.

Bear Valley was also the sight of the park headquarters, where a replica of an old Indian village had been reconstructed to simulate the life of the Miwok Indians, who had once roamed the coastal area. The village stood next to a building housing a seismograph that registered every quiver on the San Andreas fault.

"The old and the new," James murmured, "and the constant. Let's head for the Point Reyes Bird Observatory. It's not far."

The day sped by as they visited whatever took their fancy, exploring beaches where the surf crashed ominously against jagged rocks, walking sandy strands littered with shells, and hiking across pine-studded hills.

They ate a late lunch in Bodega Bay, then strolled along the shore to watch the party fishing boats come in with their catches of salmon and perch.

"What I love about this area," Diana said at one point as they walked inland from the beach through a stand of cypress, "is how undeveloped it still is. Here we are so near San Francisco yet we seem a thousand miles away."

James glanced around thoughtfully. "The place has great potential," he speculated.

A spark of annoyance flared in Diana. "Can't you see it as anything but grist for the profit mill?" she asked bitingly.

He looked at her in surprise. "Of course I can." His voice showed his resentment of her attitude. "But that doesn't mean I have to turn off the other side of my brain."

Suddenly she remembered Millie. "James," she said slowly, "what about that building your company is planning to tear down to make room for a parking lot?"

His face froze. "What about it?" he asked shortly.

"Have you really listened to the tenants?" she began, but a scowl from James stopped further words in her throat.

"What happened to our deal?" he asked coldly. "No past, remember? No future."

She turned away, her heart sinking. He was all business, wasn't he? The profit situation was what mattered most. That reminder cast a pall on the rest of their walk, but by the time they had found their car again, James's clowning had put it behind them.

They spent the rest of the afternoon exploring Fort Ross, the remnants of the North American outpost for Russion fur traders of another century. By the time they had filled themselves with history, the sun was disappearing over the ocean.

James turned the car south, and they rode in silence back toward Bodega Bay. Diana felt dread beginning to build. She didn't want this day to end. Once it was over, they would return to a time with a past and a future, and that meant decisions to be faced. And farewells.

James glanced at her as she huddled against the far door. "I don't want to go home," he said huskily. "Do you?"

The smile she turned on him was brilliant with joy. "No," she agreed. "Not yet."

"How about dinner and a walk on a moonlit beach instead?" he suggested.

"Sounds good to me." She moved closer to him across the seat.

He hadn't tried to kiss or touch her all day, but the feeling of companionship between them was strong enough to make that almost unnecessary. Yet she knew they both longed for the physical intimacy they had once shared.

CHAPTER
Nine

THE NIGHT BECAME very black before they reached their destination. They drove inland for a time, cruising through the darkened hills.

Then the ink black ocean was before them, sparkling like quicksilver under the luminous moon. The Italian restaurant they chose had tables overlooking the water, and they took their time over their shrimp scampi and veal piccata.

James's eyes looked very blue in the candlelight. Diana found herself smiling into them, unable to look away.

"James," she said at last, wanting to ask him about

his future plans, "how long are you going to be staying in San Francisco?"

"Hush," he warned her, reaching across the table to put his finger to her lips. "No past, no future. Those are the rules."

"But..."

"No." His eyes darkened as he leaned forward, and the candle's flame was reflected in his irises. "Just a woman, just a man, and endless time. That's all."

She closed her eyes as his finger caressed her cheek, then withdrew. "All right," she whispered.

The air was chilly, but they decided to walk on the sand anyway. They made their lazy way out along the margin of the bay, the sand crunching beneath their feet, the sound of the waves crashing against their ears. James slipped an arm about Diana's shoulders, holding her near, glancing down now and then to smile into her eyes, to spark the emotions she couldn't hide.

"Look!"

She pointed to a flickering light up the beach, and they both turned in that direction. A group of young people had started a huge bonfire on the sand and were sitting around it. A few of them were toasting marshmallows on sticks, laughing uproariously whenever another charred relic returned from the fire.

Diana and James watched them for a few moments, standing arm in arm at some distance, not needing to get any closer to feel the glow of the fun. With a shared smile, they moved on.

A fishy sea smell clung to the pile of rocks they were approaching. "Look out," James said, tightening his arm around her. "Watch for tidal pools."

They found a huge boulder good for leaning on and propped themselves against it, looking out to sea.

"A boat!" Diana said suddenly. "There it is." She pointed toward a small, dark vessel that moved in the night with the help of the tiniest of lights. But when she glanced up to see if James had seen it, she found him gazing down at her—and found it impossible to look away.

His hand that had been resting on her shoulder swept up to cradle her cheek, and he stared at her, his eyes serious, dark, and mysterious. He seemed to be asking her something. Without thinking, she reached for him, her hands sliding into his thick hair, pulling him down. His mouth moved across hers and warmth flowed from him, sizzling against her chilled skin and turning her shivers to trembles of delight.

She let the kiss express what she couldn't say in words, but when he seemed to say the same, she drew her lips away and said, "We really should get back."

He reared back and looked into her eyes, his own dark shadows in the night. "All in good time," he said gruffly. "We have things to do."

She knew she was crazy to let him go on with this, but before she could protest again, his mouth had caught hers, and she couldn't fight the need for him.

She kissed him with as much desire as he showed to her, and then it was she who was hot, and he cool, as his hands slipped under her sweater and caressed the heated skin of her back. The coolness felt fresh and exciting on her, and she moaned against his mouth as his fingertips brushed her sides, her ribs, then settled on her full breasts, searching for her nipple, then teasing it with his roughened thumb.

She wanted him. She wanted to devour him the way the waves devoured the shore, to take him up within her and carry him to the stars, to hold him as near as could be until the rest of forever.

"Do you remember the first time?" he whispered in her ear. "Do you remember how I held you for an hour afterward, not wanting to let your body go?"

"Oh, James!" she gasped, feeling his need. "Love me."

He groaned, and a sudden trembling shook him, but still he drew away. "Not here," he answered huskily. "Not here."

He kissed her hard, then pulled her up straight. "Come on," he told her, "let's go back to the car."

She followed him, sure that he still wanted her as much as she wanted him, but slightly puzzled by his manner. Where were they going? Just what did he have in mind?

They walked quickly now, not stopping to hear the waves or to watch the moonbeams glancing across the water. He helped her into the car, then slid behind the steering wheel. But before he started the engine, he leaned over and planted a soft kiss on her swollen lips.

"I'm going to love you, Diana," he promised, his voice still husky with passion, "but it must be right."

She didn't question him. She sat back, content to watch the trees flash by in the eerie night light as they headed back to the valley. He loved her. She was almost sure of that now. And if he didn't, he came as close to it as could be. Maybe that would be enough.

She studied his profile in the gloom, so sharply defined even in darkness, edged in gold as the light of passing headlights shot around him. Reaching out with hesitant fingers, she caressed the hair about his ear. He caught her hand, pressing a soft kiss in her palm.

"Here we are." The headlights threw their glow into the full-leafed elms, and she looked up, knowing the place, yet not recognizing it for sure in the night.

"Where?" she asked softly, peering into the darkness beyond the car lights.

James didn't speak, but turned off the lights, then sat with Diana while her eyes adjusted.

"Oh." She flashed him a quick smile of recognition.

"Lion's Mesa. You don't seriously?..."

His hand was in her hair, forcing her face back toward him. "Yes," he said in a hard voice that brought a frown to her violet eyes. "Yes, I am serious. I want to see you in the moonlight again."

She searched for the reason in his eyes, then lifted a finger and traced the line of his lips. "Let's go," she whispered. His face relaxed into a twist of a smile.

"Yes," he said simply. "Let's go."

The trail up Lion Mesa was easy to follow in the moonlight, and they scampered up it like two children, James pretending to sight mountain lions in the brush, Diana pretending to be frightened, just to please him, and both of them laughing at each other's antics.

The campsite looked just the same. They approached it quietly, as though listening for voices from the past in the breezes that tangled the leaves above them. Diana walked over and touched the huge boulder that was still such a familiar backdrop to her dreams, touched it with a hand that trembled slightly as it felt the weather-smoothed surface of the stone. The heat of the sun was still in it, radiating out to warm her fingertips, and she smiled as she pressed her hand down to draw out its secret warmth, as though it too were a ghost of an earlier sun.

Then James was behind her, his arms wrapping around her, holding in the memories, his warm mouth exploring the sensitive planes of her neck. She leaned back against him, closing her eyes and giving herself up to the sensation of a woman being loved by the man she adores.

She turned slowly in his arms, as though living a dance choreographed just for them, and when his lips found hers, his kiss was soft and tender, melting them together into a blend of woman and man, love and life. His hands were working on her body, moving slowly, creating a drowsy sensuality that carried her on in the dance, swaying with the breeze in the trees. She wound her arms about his neck, reaching high to savor all she could of his tender love, stretching her body against him in her own arabesque.

"I have waited so long for this, Diana," he breathed upon her skin, letting the warmth of his body flicker against her cheek as he spoke. "I've needed you so badly."

She couldn't speak in answer, but she moaned and twisted closer to him, welcoming the hands that began to manipulate the zipper of her slacks, helping him to rid her of them so that she stood in only her lemon yellow sweater, her long legs gleaming like fine porcelain in the silver moonlight.

Slowly he peeled back her sweater, revealing her breasts, tipped with dusky rose nipples, then her supple arms and soft shoulders. And when he had tossed the sweater and her undergarments aside, she was naked in the silver-blue night.

But she didn't give him time to savor his triumph. Urgently, she began to pull at his clothes too, needing to feel his hot skin against her own, yearning to explore the hard muscles of his firm back, his burning chest, his tightly muscled hips. And soon they were entwined on the blanket that James had brought from the car and spread on a pile of leaves.

His hands found every hidden point of sensual feeling, every place that she had saved for only him, and in the fever that sprang to vital life between them, she heard herself moaning his name over and over again.

"I need you so, James," she whispered, her voice deep and grating with the passion that seemed to fill her with a searing need to be closer, closer, ever closer. "Oh, James, love me, love me." Even she didn't know if she meant only the physical, or if it was a plea for the spiritual as well.

He was murmuring back to her, but what he said seemed to be sounds, not words, only emotion—deep, purely instinctive, and creating a response in her that came to a peak as they joined in a seal as ancient as man itself, and as fresh as each new union.

When they had spent the fury of their passion, they still clung together desperately. The wild need was sated, but the love still burned between them, and they lay together, holding on as though they would never release one another, as though they were now joined forever and would fade to nothing if separated.

A long stillness fell between them, until finally James stirred. When Diana looked up, she found him smiling down at her in the darkness.

"It is true, then," he said softly, his breath tickling her skin, still sensitive from their lovemaking. "You do exist. We did make love on a mesa under a full moon." His lips nipped playfully at her earlobe. "I must admit, at times during the last six years I was afraid I had dreamed it all. That I made it up to fill a need. That it was something I could never find again."

Diana chuckled, stretching lazily beneath him, reveling in the heaviness of his body pinning her down on the earth. "Are you going to try to make me believe there haven't been others since then?" she jeered softly, steeling herself for the answer she knew must come.

"Others?" he answered, slightly bemused. "I've been with other women, I will admit. It's been a long time. But not with many. And not one is in any way memorable. Not—" he nipped at her again—"compared to you." He grinned. "Does that satisfy you?"

It would have to. Then his eyes darkened. "And you, Diana? Not that I have any right to ask."

"No," she teased, wriggling out from underneath him. "You haven't any right." But when she saw the scowl that began to cloud his face, she reached out to touch his lips with a caressing fingertip. "Don't be silly," she chided tenderly. "How could I accept any other man after you?" She was glad it was true. After James, she had known no other man could ever move her.

With a pang, she realized his thoughts were beginning to move on to other planes. His eyes wandered. A restlessness seemed to take possession of him. She wasn't ready to lose him. Not enough had been spoken, not enough committed. He hadn't made her sure.

"There's a light on in the winery," James said, rising to stare across the valley toward the rise where Diana's house and winery stood silhouetted against the night sky. "What do you suppose is going on?"

She sat up beside him. "Gunther is probably working late getting ready for the harvest. We don't have more than a little over a week before the grapes will be ready."

He frowned. "Your equipment needs a lot of work, you know," he said chidingly. "You could be better prepared if you'd—"

"We're doing fine, thank you," she interrupted shortly. "Gunther can handle it."

James didn't seem to notice her annoyance. "I'm not so sure he can handle all the problems you've got. Yesterday when I was looking over your white wine fermentor, I found some damage to the seal. You know what oxidation will do to white wine. Gunther should be sure to have that repaired before the harvest."

Diana watched with a sinking heart as he began to dress, pulling on his shirt and his jeans. Finally she rose to do the same. It had been so good! Why couldn't that feeling last?

But something was wrong. Why was he so concerned about her equipment? It wasn't, after all, his winery. What were his plans? Did he think the deal was a foregone conclusion now, that he was sure to take over control?

Sweeter Than Wine

What a fool she was to hope for anything more. He only wanted the winery. That was clear.

Diana had no doubt that he had some feelings for her. Surely he couldn't have manufactured what they had just shared. But his feelings for his own business gains were much stronger. And she couldn't accept second place.

Though his gaze warmed a bit as she was dressing, and he reached out to help her pull her sweater on, running his hands over her breasts one last time before she covered them, he turned immediately and stared out over the vineyards. "Let's take a run over and see what Gunther is up to," he said, abstracted, not seeming to notice when Diana made no response.

Though he curled an arm about her shoulders to walk her back to the car, she felt cold inside. The golden dream that she had allowed herself to believe for just a few minutes—the one in which the two of them made love, realized that they must be together, and lived happily ever after—that dream was fading. She knew with icy certainty that more heartbreak lay ahead.

They drove back up the long drive, and when he left the car and started walking toward the winery building, she turned toward the house.

He stopped, looking after her curiously. "Where are you going?" he asked.

She took a deep breath and faced him. "The day is over, James," she said firmly, trying hard to control the tremble that threatened to creep into her voice. "We're back to reality, with its past and its future."

His face went blank as he stepped in closer. "Diana," he began, reaching for her.

"No." She stepped back, avoiding his hand. "I did as you asked. I spent a whole day with you. We explored all the aspects of our relationship, didn't we? Well I tried, but it's no good."

For a moment he looked as though he didn't know

whether to laugh or to explode in anger. "What are you trying to say, Diana?"

"I'm going up to bed, and when I get up in the morning, I hope you won't be here. It's over, James. It's time we faced facts and looked to the future."

She couldn't bear to see the hardness come back into his face, and she turned, her eyes blinded by tears, and walked quickly into the house. A part of her hoped that he would follow, that he would do something to convince her to change her mind. But there were no footsteps behind her. The house was dark and cold as she made her way to her room.

She was all right. Diana kept telling herself that over the next few days, and on a superficial level she believed it. The real heartbreak had occurred years before. She would never be hurt like that again. This time the scar protected her.

Meanwhile the chores required to prepare for the harvest took every spare minute of her time, and she had little opportunity to reflect or brood. She spent hours working in the winery, checking out equipment and finishing up the paper work.

She was working on the books one day almost a week after the night she had told James she wasn't interested in seeing him again.

"Gunther," she called out, looking from her office down the stairs into the aging cellar. "What are these papers you left out?"

Hearing no answer, she descended into the cellar, realizing he had probably climbed inside the aging tank to assure himself it was ready. Between harvests, the huge tank was always scrubbed clean, but it had to be checked periodically to be sure it was free of contamination.

Not seeing Gunther, Diana turned back into the office

Sweeter Than Wine

and picked up the pile of papers he had left strewn across the desk. They seemed to be routine forms—purchase orders, bills, and receipts. Perhaps she could just file them all away for him.

But as she rifled through the mess, a pink order form caught her eye. The slip had been attached to one describing the work they had ordered done on the barrels Gunther had taken over to the cooper. DAMAGED BEYOND REPAIR, it was stamped. *You're going to have to replace these* was jotted below the stamp in the cooper's handwriting.

Replace that many barrels? Diana sank into her chair, staring blindly at the wall. Already in debt up to their ears and overdrawn in the winery account, and now this? Despair began to well up in her throat. Without those barrels, what would they do?

Every day something new cropped up. Everywhere they turned problems waited. It seemed that each piece of property was somehow damaged, that each piece of machinery was falling apart at the same time. The budget couldn't handle it.

If they didn't get those barrels, they wouldn't be able to store and age enough wine to pay back what they already owed. The end loomed even closer than before.

Diana turned slowly as she heard Gunther enter the room. Wordlessly she held the paper up for him to see.

"Oh," he grunted, and looked away as though embarrassed.

"Oh!" she demanded. "Is that all you have to say? Oh!" She waved the paper under his nose. "Why didn't you tell me about this? What were you planning to do, spring it on me in the middle of the harvest? 'Gee, Diana, I forgot to tell you. We don't have enough barrels. Guess we might as well pour the wine out into the canyon.'"

"No." He grimaced. "It was nothing like that. I . . . I didn't think you needed to be bothered with it just now."

Diana shook her head in wonder, then said very slowly, as though tired, "But tell me, dear Gunther, how was I supposed to do anything about it if I didn't know about it?"

He sighed. "Nothing needs to be done. We have the new barrels."

She stared at him, uncomprehending. "We do? What on earth are you talking about?"

Suddenly she realized that he was flushing uncomfortably. "You didn't steal them!" she breathed, aghast.

"Don't be silly," he scoffed. "Of course I didn't steal them." He looked into her eyes and then away. "I used some of my own money," he mumbled.

"Your own money? But it must have cost you—"

"I had a little saved up," he interrupted impatiently. "I knew the winery couldn't buy them." His blue eyes glowed with a defensive blaze. "And we had to have them."

Diana stared. "You used your own money?" she whispered, at first unable to believe it. "Gunther, I . . . I don't know what to say!"

"Just say, 'Thank you, Gunther, I will pay you back some day.'" His grin was boyishly appealing. "I told you this winery is as much mine, in spirit, as it is yours. It's not a job to me, Diana. It's home."

Laughing, she jumped up and threw her arms around his neck. "I won't forget this," she promised. "Not ever." She tightened her arms around him and planted a big kiss on his pale cheek. As they both drew back laughing, a shadow in the doorway made her turn.

The laughter died in her throat when she saw it was James. His eyes were as cold as a frosty morning, and his dark, satanic expression made her whisper under her breath, "Meet the devil, Miss Kingston." She tried a smile.

"Hello, James," she said much too heartily. Flushing

slightly, she attempted a more moderate tone. "What brings you here?"

His eyes flickered over Gunther. "I'd like to talk to you, Diana."

Gunther gave her a brief smile and wordlessly left the room, while Diana steeled herself for another struggle.

James stood very still, very far away. His face was unreadable. "Diana, I want to make sure you understand me. I didn't come here to try to buy your love."

He was watching her from beneath his thick lashes in a way that made her squirm uncomfortably. "Just what did you come for?" she asked tensely.

He didn't answer, but his hard blue glance made the blood race through her veins. "Well?" She thought she would go mad if he didn't speak soon.

Something wavered in his glance, and he took a sudden, tentative step forward. "Are you sure?" he asked searchingly. "Have you thought over what you said the other night?"

She stared out the window above his shoulder. "Yes," she said firmly. "I'm sure."

He narrowed his eyes. "We were so good together, Diana," he said sharply. "How can you throw that away?"

How could she? She didn't know. But she had to. He couldn't buy her with that logic either. She pushed her hair behind her ears and glanced nervously at her desk.

"I have a pile of work to get through. Harvest is just around the corner, and this stuff can't wait. So if you'll just get to the point..."

His face hardened again. "The point, Diana, is money. Money I've got and you haven't."

She stared at him, waiting.

"I know all about the financial shape this winery is in. I've talked to some people in the city who gave me the whole picture. And I know that with your lack of resources you can't possibly take care of even the harvest you're expecting, much less pay for any other grapes to blend with. This year you stand to go even deeper in the hole. Correct?"

Still she didn't answer. She stared at him as though mesmerized.

"So," he said with a shrug, "I've come to offer you the benefit of my bank balance. What do you need to get you through this harvest?"

His eyes were so cold that she imagined him as a snake, watching her, waiting for her to move so that he would have a living target to strike for. This was it—his attempt to take control without even having to marry her.

"We don't want your money," she finally rasped out. "Get out of here."

He frowned and shook his head. "Noble rhetoric, princess, but hardly realistic. I doubt if you even have the funds to pay your pickers. With my help you can do so much more. Everything you've dreamed of." He pulled a checkbook from the vest of his suit. "How much do you need?"

She shook her head slowly, feeling her heavy hair sway against her neck and shoulders. "I'd let this winery fold before I'd take one penny of your money," she stated firmly. "Save yourself the effort of trying to persuade me. It won't work. Just put away your money and get out of here."

Anger flared in his eyes. "I'm talking about a loan, Diana. Nothing else."

She couldn't stand any more. Hands on her hips, she faced him defiantly. "James, you always come with such seductive offers. First you want to marry Lisa. Then you want to marry me. Now that those two ploys have fallen through, you think you can worm your way in by putting me in your debt. All you want is control of the winery. That's all you've ever wanted."

She was shaking, but she prayed she could hold together until she got him out the door. "Well, you can't buy my winery. Not with your love. Not with your money. Just get out."

A bewildering succession of expressions followed one another across his face, but Diana was too upset to try to read them. Suddenly he seemed to reach a decision. Curling his lip into a slight smile, he shrugged. "Have it your way, princess," he said casually, replacing the checkbook in his pocket. "But if you run into trouble you can't deal with, give me a call."

Then he was sauntering arrogantly out the door of her office. Diana sank into her chair and waited until she heard his car going down the driveway. Only when she was sure he was gone did her heartbeat return to normal.

Diana stared at the beige telephone on the old desk. In her hand was the paper on which she had written down James's telephone number and address. She was going to have to contact him somehow. But what was she going to say?

It had been almost two weeks since she had last seen him. Every hour of every day she had told herself to forget him, to concentrate on work and forget he had ever existed. But his face was tangled in her dreams, and she couldn't free herself from him.

Today the harvest should have started. She had risen before the sun had even hinted at arriving and had brewed herself a pot of strong coffee, already dressed in jeans and a sweater over a plaid shirt, ready to go into the fields to help supervise the picking of the grapes. Her first cup of coffee had barely warmed her throat when Gunther had appeared, short of breath and even shorter of temper.

"No pickers," he had announced tersely. "Not a man. Are you sure you called them for today?"

Certain that it was only a misunderstanding, she had

called the exchange, then the laborers' camp, then the local agricultural officer. No one knew anything about her pickers, the men who had promised faithfully to be there bright and early for the harvest.

By this time, Gunther had been in agony. "It's the perfect moment," he cried again and again. "We've got to move fast. Hours count! Get someone, anyone!"

She had tried. She had called every labor exchange, every organizer, the labor board, other growers. No one had any spare pickers. No one knew when any would be available.

Diana had jumped into her car and roared over the countryside, talking to people she couldn't get by phone. Still no luck. Late in the afternoon she stopped her frantic search. Sitting down in the study, she finally realized the truth.

Her own pickers had disappeared. Every other group she talked to avoided committing anyone to working for her. Something had happened. This wasn't just blind bad luck. Someone had taken control of the labor force. And she knew who that someone was.

It took a long time to decide what to do about it. To ignore him would be to let her grapes rot on the vine. If she wanted pickers, she had to go to him and demand that he release a work force for her. She had no choice.

She knew a telephone call wouldn't be sufficient. Besides, it would warn him of her approach. She had to go to him alone—now. Crushing the paper in her hand, she rose slowly and made her way to her car.

CHAPTER
Ten

THE HOUR IT took to drive into the city seemed to fly by, and then she was in the underground parking lot to James's apartment building. She took the elevator to his penthouse, then stood in the entryway, her heart in her throat.

She didn't have the proper mental attitude for this. She should rush in to confront him, livid with rage at what he had done. She should storm and accuse and show her own strength. Instead, she was trembling, scared to death.

She closed her eyes and took a very deep breath. She had to put on the facade at least.

"Yes?"

The face in the doorway startled her. It belonged to

an older man, white-haired and formal looking.

"I'd like to see Mr. Stuart," she said bravely. "Please tell him Miss Kingston is here."

He was gone for only a moment. "Mr. Stuart will see you, Miss Kingston. Please follow me."

The apartment was spacious, well lit and warm, but Diana had no eyes for the interior furnishings. The man led her out onto a sundeck that wrapped around a sparkling blue pool, which looked inviting even in the fading light of evening. Alongside, stretched back on a chaise, sat James with Dictaphone, papers, and pens beside him. His white swimming trunks showed off the tan on his long, brown legs, and the unbuttoned pale blue shirt he wore revealed the dark matted hair of his chest.

He didn't rise as she came near, and his eyes were as impenetrable as a foggy day. The man who had led her outside turned back toward the house, and Diana was left to face James alone.

She stared at him, unable to summon the anger the occasion deserved, but determined to do what must be done.

"You did it, didn't you?" she said finally, her voice surprising her in its firmness.

His thin smile showed that he wasn't going to waste any time with phony denials. "Of course," he answered simply.

She took another deep breath. "What do I have to do to get you to release a work force to me?"

"What makes you think you could persuade me to do that?"

She shook her head, swirling her hair around her shoulders. Her eyes didn't leave his. "Even you wouldn't be so hard as to let a whole crop be destroyed," she said quietly.

He raised one dark eyebrow sardonically. "You think not?" he asked. He gestured toward a chair that stood next to the chaise. "Sit down and we'll talk about it."

She clenched her hands into fists at her sides. "I don't want to talk. I want my pickers."

His gaze held hers. "Sit down," he demanded, his voice icy.

Very slowly she did as he had ordered, then she glared at him rebelliously. "Why are you doing this to me?" she asked tautly.

His smile was lazy, his eyes hooded. "You think I'm very hard, don't you, Diana? You think I go through life as ruthlessly as a pirate, grabbing what I want and slashing the proverbial throats of all opponents, don't you?"

She nodded. "That's a pretty fair picture," she told him crisply. "Here I am, Exhibit A. A bleeding victim."

His laugh was low and humorless. "Thanks a lot, Diana," he said tonelessly. "I asked for a little faith. Was that too much to give?"

She frowned, not sure what he was driving at. "I'm really not interested in philosophical discussions," she insisted stubbornly. "I just want my pickers."

He shook his head sadly, gazing at her, and sighed. "I guess I can't really expect anything more," he said as though to himself. "Have you tried to get pickers somewhere else? Did you stop by the labor exchange?"

"You know I did."

He nodded confidently. "Did you try to get pickers from your neighbors and friends?"

She gritted her teeth. "Yes."

"And you had no luck in any of those places?"

She didn't bother to answer him.

"Well, Diana, it looks as though I have you in a real bind, doesn't it? You must get your harvest in, but you can't do it without pickers. Right?"

Her anger finally exploded. "You know all that. Why do you have to rub it in? What kind of man are you? You have me crawling to you. What more can you want?"

He looked into the blue-green water of the pool. Night had fallen completely now and the pool light was on, lending an eerie atmosphere to the poolside deck. "I'm not trying to torture you, Diana," he said quietly. "I have my reasons for doing this."

"I'm sure you do," she retorted. "I'm sure you have great reasons for all the things you do. What did you want, revenge? Did you want to make me miserable for turning down your deals? Okay. You've got it. I'm miserable."

He turned his head to look at her, and he shook his head. "Diana, the last thing in the world I want is to make you miserable. Don't you understand that?"

"No." Her voice was low and angry. "I don't understand that at all."

"Then listen to me and you soon will." He sat up straight in his chair. "I have control of the pickers. You've admitted that. Don't you think that I could also control other things around you if I wanted to?"

"What do you mean?" she breathed.

"If I wanted to destroy your irrigation system, Diana, I could get your water supply revoked. If I wanted to turn the coopers against you, I could. Or any of the suppliers you depend on. Or the banks."

Diana went cold. What was he suggesting?

"Don't you see?" he said. "I put on this little show of strength for one reason. I wanted to give you a graphic demonstration of how I could squeeze you out at any time. There are a hundred ways I could do it. If I really wanted your winery, all I would have to do is employ the means at my disposal and soon you would have to sell."

It was true. She could see how vulnerable she was. But what was his point?

"Diana, Diana." He looked as though he wanted to reach out for her, but was holding himself back. Instead, he rose and stood over her. "I don't need to marry you to get your winery. I don't need to bribe you or buy you in any way. I've got the power to do it much more easily, if I choose."

She was blinking at him, not really sure if she understood what he was trying to say.

His hands came up to cradle her face. "I don't want your winery, you little fool," he said fiercely. "All I've ever wanted was you."

He wanted to kiss her, but she wasn't ready for that.

"Wait." Her hands were on his chest, holding him back. "You mean, you don't want my winery?"

"No." His hands tightened on her as though he would like to shake her. "I don't want your winery."

"But you told me you did that day in your office."

A dark look shadowed his face. "I said a lot of ugly things that day. I was still hurt over what happened six years ago. I wanted revenge."

There it was again, the mystery. This time she musn't let him avoid telling her just what had hurt him. "Why do you want revenge, James?" she cried. "What have you held against me all this time?"

He looked startled. "I think you know," he growled.

"No," she insisted, "that's just the point. I *don't* know at all."

He frowned as though he didn't quite believe her, then dropped his hands and turned back to sit down on the chaise. "Maybe it would be better if we talked about it," he agreed.

He stared into the pool again. "Six years. So long ago. Yet it feels like yesterday." His smile was thin.

She watched him thinking over the past and felt her hands gripping one another tightly in her lap. Was she finally going to learn the truth? If only he would speak!

Finally he looked up at her, his eyes bright and searching. "The night before that last day, we made love so thoroughly that I thought we'd formed a connection that could never be broken. I was so sure you loved me."

He stopped, and she still waited. Yes, she had loved him. But what about him? What had he felt for her?

"You wanted to get married, and I agreed. Anything to keep you with me. You wanted to announce our engagement at your party." He turned to stare at her with tortured eyes. "Do you remember how we argued about that? How I wanted to wait? And you... you laughed and said no, that you wanted to show your parents how deep our love was so they couldn't object." His laugh split the air like a sliver of ice. "Do you remember?"

She nodded. Somehow she couldn't speak.

He shook his head in bewildered exasperation, frowning. "Then can you give me one good explanation for what happened? Why you changed your mind?"

Now she was angry. "One good explanation! For what? For not understanding that you could love me one night, then leave with that... that *person* the next day? For not being tolerant enough to accept that you didn't want to come to my party..."

"I was planning to attend that party, Diana, just as we had agreed. I went out and bought myself a suit. I had just come in from working and was about to go over to the showers when your father showed up at my camp with your message."

She shook her head. "But I didn't send you any message."

His smile was crooked. "Don't you remember?"

She frowned. She couldn't think of any reason why she might have sent her father with a message. "No," she insisted.

He searched her face, a strange light appearing in his eyes. "You didn't send your father?"

"James, I'm sure I didn't. What did he say?"

He shook his head slowly. "It doesn't matter," he

Sweeter Than Wine

murmured. Then a bittersweet smile softened his mouth. "No," he added decisively. "That's in the past. And what we are concerned with is the present."

He was standing before her again, reaching down to pull her up. "The important thing is that you believe I don't have designs on your winery. You do believe that now, don't you?"

She wanted to believe him. Looking in his deep blue eyes, she was ready to believe anything he said. But the doubts still clung.

"You must admit you show an awful lot of interest for someone who doesn't want to take over," she reminded him. "Every time I turn around, you're delving into all the operations."

A look of astonishment flashed across his face and was gone. "But of course," he explained. "The winery business is new to me and I'm fascinated by it. Whenever I go into a venture, I throw myself into it without reservation. That's just the way I am."

She knew it was part of his character, and she accepted that. But still...

"If what you say is true, why did you want to marry Lisa?"

He smiled. "I wanted to hurt you. I wanted to be near you. It was very confused, even in my mind, but it all involved you."

Could she trust him? How she wanted to!

"Diana, don't you see? When I finally came back to this country, I had to see you again. I didn't know if you would even remember me. And if you did, I was afraid you might despise me. But I had to find out. And when I met Lisa, the way was cleared."

"But you didn't have to get close to marrying her." That was still a sticking point.

He laughed, pulling her close. She knew he was beginning to sense victory.

"That almost engaged silliness was all Lisa's doing. She brought it up, and I didn't discourage her, but neither of us ever took it seriously." He leaned down to kiss the top of Diana's head.

"Did you know that Gunther is in love with Lisa?" Diana whispered, letting her arms slowly make their way around his waist, feeling the warm skin as his shirt fell away.

"Oh, yes." He chuckled. "Did you know that *Lisa* is pretty much in love with *Gunther?*"

Diana pulled back, startled. "What? Where did you get that idea?"

His smile caressed her neck before he bent to drop a kiss there. "I got that idea from Lisa herself. Gunther is all she talks about."

"Really? I wonder why she never mentioned it to me. He's so totally different from any of the other men she dates."

James nuzzled her ear, making tiny prickles start a dance down the sensitive side of her neck. "And how many of them did she ever love?" he challenged. "His being different can only be in his favor."

"But . . . then why don't they just get together? They have every chance!"

He raised his head and shrugged. "The guy is not one of your truly aggressive types. I think that was one of the reasons Lisa decided to play around with me for a while. She thought it might wake him up."

Diana smiled as she slipped into James's embrace again. "You know, I think it just might have worked." Her fingers found the solid muscular wall of his back and began moving on it, sensing where to massage firmly, where to brush softly.

The night sky was black, and the only light was the one shining under the water of the pool. The air seemed to be cooling off, but Diana couldn't be sure. A delicious warmth was surging through her, flowing down to tingle the ends of her fingers and the tips of her toes. She was drifting in drowsy excitment, and when James's lips sought hers, she welcomed them, welcomed the tongue that flickered over her mouth and then entered to explore the warm wetness of her surrender.

"Do you believe me now?" His whisper was another caress, slightly rough but warming, exciting. "Do you believe that all I ever wanted was you?"

She felt laughter rising from deep inside her. She *did* believe it. "I might need a little more convincing," she teased, rubbing her face against the hair that matted his chest. "Why don't you try your hand at it?"

"With pleasure," he growled, his mouth against her hair, and then his hands were sliding in under her blouse, pulling it free from her slacks and covering the bare skin of her back with his spread fingers.

She knew she was probably crazy to trust him. He had betrayed her before, and when she asked for explanations, all she got were vague mutterings about what she had done to him. They still sounded like rationalizations to her. And a man who had made that sort of betrayal once could very well do it again.

But still, she no longer suspected him of ulterior motives. He really did want her. For how long? Did it matter? She would have to learn to live in the present. That was all she had.

He unbuttoned her blouse and began to unfasten the clasp of her bra. She arched against him like a cat in a sunny window, desiring him with all the fire he could ask for.

His mouth descended, blazing a trail of heat along the line of her chin, down the sinews of her throat, curving out along her collarbone, then down to capture first one naked nipple, then the other, drawing them fully erect with the coaxing of his agile tongue, then nipping with his teeth until she writhed with the agony of wanting him.

She drew his face back up to hers again, drinking in the nectar of his kiss, reveling in the feel of her breasts against the rough texture of the hair on his chest, thrilling to the evidence of his need for her as he pressed his long length to her.

He pulled away, and she met his gaze boldly as his eyes lingered on her naked shoulders and shapely breasts gleaming in the strange, glowing light from the pool.

"You're more beautiful than ever," he said huskily, his hands on her shoulders. "Don't ever doubt me again, Diana. I've never wanted any other woman as I've wanted you."

Before she could answer, a voice rang out through the night air. "Is there anything else you desire before I say good night, Mr. Stuart?"

Diana froze against James, horrified. She had forgotten all about the man who worked here. Embarrassment sweeping over her, she hid her face against James's chest, vividly aware of her naked back, and of her shirt and bra strewn about in plain sight.

James tightened his hold on her. "No thank you, Benton. That will be all for this evening. Please feel free to retire for the night."

"Very well, sir." And the man was gone.

"Oh, I hate you!" Diana was beating on his naked chest with ineffectual blows from her fists and laughing as she spoke. "I've never been so embarrassed before in my life!"

He caught her hands, laughing along with her. "Don't worry," he chortled. "Benton is very discreet. He didn't see a thing. When it comes to this sort of escapade, he is blind, deaf, and dumb."

"I see." Suddenly the humor went out of the situation. "I guess he gets a lot of practice at that, doesn't he?"

Sweeter Than Wine

She drew away from him and began to reach for her clothes.

"Hey." He leaned forward to stop her. "What do you think you're doing?"

"Getting out of here," she announced. "I can't do this sort of thing with an audience."

Laughing, he forced her back into his arms. "Benton has gone to bed. He won't be back. I promise."

She looked around nervously. "You're sure?"

He kissed her temple. "I'm positive. But just to be safe..."

With one swift movement he swept her up, his arm under her knees, and began carrying her into the house.

"Where are we going?" She squirmed in his embrace, afraid of whom they might meet.

"My bedroom," he told her firmly. "With a lock on the door and all the modern conveniences."

She relaxed against him, snuggling her face into the hollow of his shoulder. "All right," she whispered.

He strode quickly through his large living room and carried her into a room decorated in various shades of blue. Lowering her gently onto the royal blue quilted spread, he stopped above her, letting his gaze run over her naked flesh.

As his hands began to work at the clasp of her jeans, she lay back drowsily, watching him through half-closed eyes, loving the desire that flamed in his eyes whenever they met hers.

"This time it will be in my own bed," he told her huskily as he stripped off his pants and lay down beside her. "And this time I'm going to make you mine, sweet Diana. No more doubts."

His hands were stroking, searching, testing, igniting a thousand tiny fires all over her skin. She writhed beneath him, captured by his spell, reaching for him and moaning his name.

"Love me, James," she coaxed hoarsely. "Love me now."

"I do love you, Diana," he said, his mouth against her hair, "and I will, forever."

The weight of his body as he came down on her was exquisitely confining, and her hands clutched at his muscular back, urging him on. Their movements matched in the dance of love, sending her senses spiraling higher, until she cried out in sweet agony, and he met her demand with one of his own. The summit was reached, and the long, delicious slide back down lasted long enough to bring them both up smiling.

Diana sighed her happiness, meeting his descending lips with a lazy kiss.

"Did you like that, princess?" he teased her. "That was only a sample. You stick around, and I'll provide you with a lifetime supply."

"Name your price," she drawled, running her fingers through his impossibly thick hair. "I think I'm addicted."

A laugh rumbled deep in his throat. "Guess what," he chided her. "All that, and we didn't even lock the door."

She turned to look at it. "You're right," she admitted ruefully. "I guess we got caught up in other concerns."

She half rose to look at him as he lay back. His body was so hard and dark, she couldn't keep from touching him, exploring every ridge and bulge with her fingers. He had said he loved her, and she knew that in a way it was true. He had shown her how much he cared. But was it enough to keep him this time? Was it enough to risk it all again? She wasn't sure.

His large hand came up and caught at the back of her head. "You're going to stay with me tonight, aren't you?" he asked languorously. "In fact, why not just send for your things and stay for good. We could live in here for days with Benton to run our errands."

Sweeter Than Wine

She grinned and leaned down to run a line of kisses along his breastbone between the two wings of his ribcage, letting her hair brush his skin. Then the swirl of wiry hairs around his navel attracted her, and she visited them with her tongue.

"You know I have to go," she said regretfully. "And you have work to do too."

He pulled her back down on top of him, reaching up to kiss her soundly. "Don't worry," he said gruffly. "Your harvest will proceed tomorrow. And I'll come over to lend you a hand." His kiss deepened, and he sighed when their lips separated again. "But I want you to stay right now. I need you to stay."

She looked down at his face, and the love she felt for him swept over her, making her speechless for a moment. She knew how shaky the foundations of her happiness were. He had walked out on her before, and he would very likely do so again. But at least she had this. And right now, what else mattered?

"I'll stay for a while," she agreed. "But I must go back tonight. Promise?"

His arms tightened around her, drawing her hard against his body. "I promise," he whispered as he began a new assault upon her senses.

CHAPTER
Eleven

SHE HADN'T FELT the need to ask him about her pickers. She had known they would arrive the next morning. And so she assured a very nervous Gunther, though he didn't believe her at first.

"I can't understand how anyone would stoop so low as to try this sort of trick," he fumed, pacing about Diana as she drank her early morning coffee. "He wants to ruin us, that's all."

"No," she answered, her soft eyes glazed with a faraway look. "He doesn't want to ruin us. He's coming to help us himself. You'll see."

Gunther threw a worried look her way, and she wondered if he could tell just how different her attitude toward James was. She was tempted to tell him, but thought better of it. He'd be able to see for himself shortly.

"Is Lisa coming out to pick?" he asked suddenly.

Lisa had been visiting friends in Laguna Beach for the last week, but she always came home for the harvest and had arrived some time the day before. It was a family tradition. Not only was it customary, it was also necessary, for any extra pair of hands was always welcome.

Lisa had returned, but she and Gunther had been involved in some sort of argument that Diana didn't fully understand and as a result, Lisa had refused to join them this morning.

"She may come along later," Diana hedged, amused by the look of pained disgust Gunther threw her.

The two of them went out into the still dark vineyards. For a few anxious moments they waited in the chilly gloom, pacing back and forth, hugging their arms in tight against the cold. Then the headlights of several trucks appeared on the highway, and soon the noise of the engines came rumbling across the fields, growing louder and closer, until they rolled to a stop near where the two watchers stood. Quietly, almost as though in deference to the still of the day, the men began to descend and pick up their equipment. A car from the head of the convoy stopped nearby and James stepped out of it.

"Good morning," he greeted Diana as they both stood in the dawn haze, the cool morning dew still thick in the air.

She smiled and tried to walk past him, but he reached out and gathered a handful of her hair, brought his face down to barely kiss it, and gazed at her meaningfully. "You're as lovely in the dark of morning as you are in the dark of night," he said in a low voice that was barely above a whisper.

She flushed, loving the words and the emotion that triggered them. "Quiet," she admonished playfully. "This is business."

Gunther had seen their exchange, and he glared resentfully in James's direction. "We have work to do, Diana," he said huffily, and she shot James a quick, secret glance before hurrying over to join the vintner.

The pickers were a good crew. Many of them had worked these vineyards before, and they went about their work quickly and efficiently.

They deftly cut each cluster of succulent fruit from its stem and tossed it into a square bin that every picker had with him. When that was full, it was emptied into a large gondola on a truck at the side of the road, soon to be rushed to the crusher at the winery. The men worked fast and since there were quite a few of them, the work progressed nicely, promising an early culmination of the year's effort.

"What's he doing here?" Gunther snorted at one point, casting a poisonous glance at James. "I thought he was into sabotage, not helping."

Diana smiled. Gunther would need time to forgive the incident with the pickers. But when he did, she hoped he and James would become friends. James was going to be around a lot from now on. She was counting on that. She didn't let herself think about what she would do when he grew tired of her.

"He's keeping an eye on his future investment, I imagine," she answered glibly.

"More likely he's putting his curse on it," Gunther grumbled. He looked at Diana searchingly. "Are you going to let him buy in?" he demanded.

Looking him straight in the eye, she smiled. "Yes, Gunther. We need the money."

He shook his head hopelessly. "This is the end," he prophesied with gloom, but Diana was surprised that he reacted so calmly. Even Gunther seemed finally to accept that they had reached the end of the road.

The sun began to beat down their heads, and the

workers made more and more excuses to drink from the canteens and beverage jugs. Groups dropped off from time to time to devour a quick midmorning snack, but everyone was soon back at work, hoping to finish before the heat of late afternoon.

Diana looked up occasionally to find James's eyes on her, and often she was startled by the intensity of his stare. Sometimes she was chilled by the look she saw in his eyes. But whenever he came close, his manner was all she could wish for.

"Do you remember," he said once when he passed her, "the time you had car trouble just beyond that curve?"

She refused to meet his eyes, embarrassed to recall her obvious ploy, but a smile fluttered on her lips.

His fingers curled around her upper arm, stroking a tantalizing message. "I knew then that I had to have you at all costs," he growled so near her ear that she could feel his warm breath stir the hair that hung there. She glanced up and caught the odd look in his eyes again.

"But even now I don't have all of you," he said, his voice bemused. "When do I get it all, Diana?"

She stared at him, astounded, as he walked on across the field. What on earth was he talking about? She had given him everything a woman could. She couldn't imagine what he meant.

The sun was hanging low in the afternoon sky when the work began to slow. Diana's hair hung in tangled strands and she knew her face was streaked with dirt, but she was floating on a cloud of success. They'd made it. They'd fought off the deer, the birds, even the bees, had weathered the thunderstorms, the freezes, the wind and rain, had survived the late summer heat wave. The grapes were in.

Closing her eyes, she leaned her head back in a tiny,

thankful prayer, then looked up to meet Gunther's jubilant grin.

"Oh boy, oh boy!" he was repeating again and again. "This is it. This is really it!"

They had planned to go immediately to the winery to get on with the wine making, but before they could make a start for it, a honking sounded on the road.

"Wait, everyone," Lisa was calling, jumping from the cab of the winery pickup truck. "We've brought you all supper."

Tired workers moved with renewed energy when they saw the feast in store for them, and very soon the boards and sawhorses Lisa and Mrs. Cruz had brought from the house were set up as makeshift tables. Red-and-white checkered cloths looked positively festive covering the raw wood, and when the huge platters of barbecued chicken pieces were placed on it, there were sighs of anticipation all around.

Mrs. Cruz had roasted corn on the cob and baked her special seed-and-cheese supper loaf to go with the chicken, and Lisa had cut cantaloupe into wedges, which she wrapped with strips of salami. Gallon jugs of chilled white picnic wine rounded out the meal.

"This is just what we needed," Diana enthused as she filled her plate with food. "I didn't realize how hungry I was until I smelled this."

"You can thank your sister," Mrs. Cruz commented as she poured wine into cups. "This was all her doing."

"I thought you might be able to use a pick-me-up before going on to the winery," Lisa agreed. She glanced under her thick eyelashes at Gunther. "You see, I do know something about how to take care of vintners."

Gunther looked up, startled, but he retreated into his meal again when he encountered Lisa's downcast eyes. Watching the exchange, Diana shook her head in despair.

"He still doesn't have the secret, does he?" James whispered into her ear. He was sitting beside her, and she enjoyed the warm companionship they were sharing. "He doesn't know when the woman is giving him a clear signal to join battle."

Diana threw him an ironic smile. "And I suppose you do?" she challenged. "I suppose you always know what a woman means by every sign she sends?"

"Of course I do." His superior smile was infuriating. "I won you over, didn't I? And you know you were a formidable foe."

She smiled as he slipped an arm around her shoulders. But inside was a question struggling to get out, a question she didn't dare put into words: now that you've won me, what do you intend to do with your prize? Why couldn't she ask him that? Why was she so afraid of the answer?

Pleasantly stuffed, they began to leave the table and gather the last of the grapes for the trek up the hill. Gunther was bouncing again, so excited by the good harvest. "This is the best ever," he was saying to anyone who would listen. "This is it."

His feelings of euphoria were infectious, and as he bounded near, Diana laughed and threw a playful punch at his dirty shoulder. "Okay, vintner," she chortled. "Let's go make our wine."

She turned to draw James into the joyful celebration, and the three of them started the long walk home, while the others piled into the waiting trucks.

When Diana first left the fields, exhaustion slowed her steps, but by the time the wine making was well under way, new enthusiasm filled her. Excitement filled the air. Everyone was smiling; everyone's eyes were bright with hopeful expectation.

Sweeter Than Wine

Gunther seemed to think this would certainly be a banner year. He couldn't resist testing the must, the unfermented juice just pressed from the grapes. As he made his rounds of the tanks, his saccharometer, the instrument with which he tested the sugar level of the juice, revealed that the content was at a level perfect for the making of fine wine. The acidity was within a tolerable range as well, and Gunther walked about beaming like a new father.

"Ambrosia, ambrosia! Here, have a taste!"

Everyone was sipping the fresh grape juice and glowing with pride, and Diana and James were swept up in their delight. They spent hours testing and adding the yeast to begin fermentation. When it was finally time to stop, the first violet light of morning was spreading pale streaks across the sky.

Diana walked out with James as he strode toward his car.

"I want to thank you for all your help," she said awkwardly. His face looked haggard in the light of the new dawn, and she longed to reach out and push back the wayward strand of hair that fell over his forehead. But he was looking at her in that strange way again, and she didn't dare.

He stopped and stared down at her without smiling. "You don't have to thank me for anything," he said in a strained voice. "Not ever."

Puzzled as to what he could possibly mean by that, she started to speak, but he silenced her by placing a finger on her lips. "We have to talk, Diana," he said in a low, tired voice. "But not now. I'll call you after I've had some sleep."

Suddenly his face was near hers, and his mouth was gently teasing her lips apart with a kiss that sent her heart pounding in her chest. With one hand he pulled her close against him, pressing her yielding body to the length of him. With the other he held her chin captive as he explored her warm response.

But when he pulled away, it was almost in anger, and he strode to his car without looking back. She stared after him, wondering just what was happening between them. Had he begun to have second thoughts? No, something in her cried. Not yet.

But she wouldn't think about that. She was tired, too, and needed to sleep. It would be better in the morning.

Diana slept well enough. As soon as she rose, she ran back down to the winery to see how matters stood. The frantic pace of the previous day had given way to a more leisurely tempo. No snags had developed; everything was going smoothly. The harvest had been a success, and so had the crush. Now they would have to wait to see how well the fermentation had gone.

Still, Gunther seemed strangely perturbed.

"What is it?" Diana asked him after enduring one too many of his sarcastic remarks. "I'd think you would be in a rosier mood today. After all, the harvest was smooth, the crush successful. What's the problem?"

He flashed her a withering look without a verbal answer, and she was forced to assume that he was feeling let down after all the excitement of the past few days.

She took care of some bookkeeping, then found herself staring at the walls, wishing James would call, wishing she had something to do to keep her mind off him.

"Did you know that your sister is gone again?" Gunther grumbled at one point as he poked his nose into her office.

Diana raised her head in surprise. "No! When did she leave?"

"This morning while you were still sleeping. She went

Sweeter Than Wine

off to play tennis with that Tony Jordan." His frown was deeper than ever. "He's supposedly leaving for the Middle East tonight." His snort of disbelief gave ample evidence that he considered that merely a ruse, and Diana hid a smile.

"Did she say when she'd be back?"

"No. Maybe she won't be back. Maybe..." he shot another crusty glance her way "...maybe she'll run off to Saudi Arabia with this Tony fellow."

Diana laughed. "That won't happen, and you know it." She turned to look into his face. "Have you told her yet?"

He knew exactly what she meant. "No," he grunted.

She shrugged. "Then you can hardly blame her for going out with someone else." Her eyes narrowed as she gazed at him. "Go tell her right now," she ordered.

"What?" He looked startled.

"Yes." She warmed to her idea. "Go over to the tennis club, walk out onto the court, and tell her right there in front of everyone."

He stared at her. "You're crazy," he said finally.

She nodded. "Of course I'm crazy. The whole idea's crazy. That's what's so wonderful about it."

Standing up, she looked intently into his eyes. "You're a winner, Gunther. You've just brought in one hell of a harvest. You can do this too."

A smile curled up into his pale blue eyes. "Right out in front of everyone?" he asked breathlessly, excitement showing on his face.

She nodded. "Right now," she encouraged.

He began hunting in his pockets for his car keys. "I'll just go over there," he said as though reassuring himself. "I'll just see how things are going."

"That's right," she coaxed, pushing him out the door. "Just go over there."

She smiled as she watched him drive down the road. "Good luck," she whispered. Then her thoughts returned to her own problems.

Mindless busy work was all she could find to do, and she knew she was only doing it to keep her mind from the telephone call she was aching to receive. Somehow she had decided James was planning to call her today, and when hour followed hour and still the phone remained mute before her, it became all she could think about.

The hours were spinning by. She could stand the suspense no longer. Steeling her courage, she reached for the telephone and dialed James's number.

The phone rang and rang, and she finally had to accept the fact that he wasn't home. With a shrug of exasperation, she tried the number at his office.

Though his secretary was reluctant, she put the call through, and Diana was embarrassed by the warmth that spread through her veins at the sound of his rich voice.

"Hello, Diana." She heard affection there. She couldn't be imagining it. "I'm sorry I haven't called you, but I've been awfully busy on a special project."

"I was wondering... are you going to be stopping by tonight?" Oh Lord! She sounded so tentative, almost as though she were pleading. She couldn't allow herself to be put in this position!

But she still had hopes—which were soon dashed by his words.

"No... listen, Diana. I'm really sorry, but this project ... I've got something I want to take care of before I see you again."

"I see." Her tone was icy now. She wanted him to know that she would appreciate a fuller explanation. But he didn't seem to hear the displeasure in her voice.

"I'll give you a call."

"All right."

Sweeter Than Wine   171

The hand that placed the receiver carefully back into its cradle was cold and stiff. Was she losing him again? Had she ever really had him?

Brushing those thoughts aside, she returned to the house and set about preparing a complicated dinner to keep her thoughts off James as much as possible.

An hour later she was startled by the sound of the front doorbell. Gunther would walk right in; so would her sister. Could it be James?

She rushed to the door, a smile of welcome ready on her face, which was flushed from cooking. But to her disappointment, her visitor was Millie Bradshaw.

"My goodness, you don't have to look so glad to see me," Millie teased at Diana's crestfallen expression.

"But I am glad to see you," Diana countered, inviting Millie into the house. "I was just...I thought maybe you were someone else."

"Ah-ha! Someone special, is it? And who might that be?"

Diana evaded the issue. "No one, really. Come on into the study and tell me what has brought you all the way out here at this time of day."

"Exciting news!" The older woman fairly bubbled with it, but she refused to explain until they both were seated in the study with steaming cups of tea.

"I braved the lion today and came out a winner," she declared at last.

Diana smiled, enjoying the sparkle Millie projected. "And who was this lion?" she asked curiously.

"James Stuart, of course."

Diana felt her smile freeze. "What are you talking about?"

"It's all your fault, really," Millie bubbled on. "If you hadn't involved me with those people and their housing protests, it never would have happened."

"Will you please be a little more explicit?" Diana

laughed. "I'd like to be bursting with happiness along with you, but I can't until I know what this is all about."

"You do remember that we were going to picket James Stuart for planning to tear down an apartment house and build a parking garage? Well, we did it every day last week and got nowhere. James refused to meet with us. The plans were going through to evict everyone. I knew I had to do something for those poor people."

Diana frowned. "But what could you do? If the picketing didn't affect them—"

"You know what I could do. I know James Stuart personally. I could corner him on my own."

Diana grinned, wishing she had been there. "You didn't!"

Millie nodded proudly. "I did. And what's more, it worked."

Diana gasped, delighted. She remembered how adamant James had been about the issue. "What did you use, magic?"

"Nope. Just good old common sense. And he bought it. But that's not all. He's also agreed to look into ways of making it more livable for the people there. Better security, more recreational facilities on the premises."

"Now just how did you work this miracle?" Diana asked, thoroughly surprised. She loved James, but she knew he was a hard businessman who didn't give away anything for nothing.

Millie smirked, obviously well pleased with herself. "I've been working on plans for the last two weeks. I got everything all together—cost estimates, projected use factors, all the goodies I could think of—and presented it all to him as a business person should. I admitted the costs involved, the lost revenues from the parking structure. But I balanced that against the public relations benefit for his firm. I mapped out a p.r. campaign that knocked his socks off. 'You're out there buying adver-

Sweeter Than Wine 173

tising,' I told him, 'spending millions. You can write this off the same way. And benefit your own community while you're at it.'"

"And he bought it!"

"Not only did he buy it, he also hired me to coordinate the whole business."

Diana laughed. "Millie! Oh, darling!" Jumping up, she pulled the woman to her feet and hugged her tightly.

"Isn't that something? Millie Bradshaw, public relations coordinator. And here I thought my life was over."

Was this the project James had been talking about, Diana wondered. Was this the reason he couldn't see her tonight? She hoped so.

Millie stayed for quite some time, so thrilled by the turn her life was taking that she needed to go over and over the details, her plans, her dreams. Diana tried to talk her into staying for dinner, but she claimed to be too excited to eat. Finally, as she began to gather herself in preparation for leaving, Diana had a sudden thought.

"Millie," she said slowly, "do you remember the summer after I graduated from high school? The year Lisa went to Europe with Aunt Margery?"

Millie pursed her lips. "I certainly do. That was the year the birds nearly ruined our harvest. Herbert was out there every day, tying up tin foil, bells, wind chimes. He even bought three battery-operated record players and put them out in the fields to play animal noises to try to keep those pesky—"

"I remember that," Diana interjected impatiently. "But do you remember anything about Daddy being upset with me over some fellow I was crazy about? Does anything like that ring a bell for you?"

She watched her old friend's face intently, for she knew her father would have shared anything upsetting him with Millie and Herbert. They had been her parents' closest friends.

Millie's face was creased with thought, then a light seemed to go off behind her gray eyes.

"Oh, sure. You were chasing after some field hand that summer."

"Millie! I was hardly chasing after him!"

"Oh, honey, don't get your dander up. We all chase after someone at that age. If we waited around for the lazy things to..." She put a quick end to that train of thought as she saw the impatience flicker in Diana's eyes once again. "Anyway," she went on hastily, "yes, I remember it well. Your father came to us, heartsick and angry. You'd told him you wanted to marry someone they didn't know, and when he checked on who you'd been seeing, he found it was one of his own workers. I told him at the time that it was pure foolishness, that you were too bright and on the ball to waste your life that way. Why, you still had four years of college and all..."

"Millie, please. Did he tell you what he was going to do about it?"

She nodded. "Sure. He was planning to forbid you to see this person ever again. He was going to fire the boy and lock you in your room."

That rang absolutely true. It was just the sort of thing her father would have done. "But he didn't do those things. Why not?"

"We talked him out of it." Millie chuckled. "As I told him, the best way to drive his headstrong daughter straight into that boy's arms was to forbid it. Happens every time."

Diana's stomach was lurching and a cold sweat was beading her forehead. "I see," she said shakily.

"Go directly to the boy himself, I told your father. Give him some incentive to pack his bags and move on out. She'll forget him in a week." Suddenly Millie looked sharply at Diana. "Why are you asking this, honey? What exactly did happen that summer?"

Diana tried to smile. "Oh, Dad followed your advice. He got rid of the boy, just as you told him to."

So it was true. Her father had gone to James and talked him into leaving. But how had he done that? What could he have told James that could possibly have convinced him to leave her the way he had?

"Well, I guess it worked out fine," Millie chattered on. "You went off and had your college years and turned out just perfect, didn't you?" She rose and gave her younger friend a swift kiss. "And now I must be off. I have plans to make, people to see. Isn't it exciting?"

Diana saw Millie to the door, then wandered slowly back through the house. Her mind was filled with pictures—scenes of the time she had spent with James that summer, scenes of talks with her parents, scenes of her party. They all whirled through her in a mass of confusion that sent her nerves into chaos.

James had been telling the truth all this time. He hadn't left of his own free will. Her father had done something that made him leave. She had to know what it was.

How could her father have done this to her? She had been young, certainly, and headstrong. And he had been right to worry. But he had done something terrible. . . . She had to find out what.

She must talk to James about it. Suddenly she knew that once they cleared this up, the nightmare would finally end. Hope surged again. She was sure this time.

Dinner would have to wait. She turned off the warming flame and reached for the kitchen telephone, dialing as she shrugged into her jacket. The switchboard was closed at the office building, and the night watchman assured her that everyone had gone. Her call to the apartment didn't receive an answer either. Well, he had to go home sometime. She hung up and hurried toward the door.

She raced the Triumph over the country roads and the black-topped highway onto the freeway, then down over the Golden Gate Bridge. Excitement coursed through her at the thought of seeing James again. She was glad she had decided to take the chance.

It felt very late by the time she rolled into the basement parking lot of his building. The elevator quickly took her to the penthouse floor, but no one answered when she rang the bell. A cold feeling was numbing her bones. Where on earth could he be?

She looked at her watch and decided that waiting would only drive her crazy. A building manager was listed on the directory. Perhaps he would have a clue as to the whereabouts of his most important tenant.

It turned out that James was not exactly a tenant. "Mr. Stuart? Sure I know him," the gray-haired man chortled as he held open the door to his small apartment. "He owns the building; I better know him!"

"Do you have any idea where I might find him tonight?"

He looked at her suspiciously, then seemed to decide she must be on the up and up. "Tell you the truth," he said slowly, "I kind of figured he was going out of town. He takes a lot of business trips overseas, you know. In fact, he only recently moved his living quarters here."

"Yes, I know." James hadn't mentioned a trip. "But wouldn't he inform you if that were the case?"

The building manager shrugged. "Usually, but not always. It doesn't make much of a difference in my workload whether he's here or not." He looked at Diana keenly. "And I do know that he gave that Benton fellow who works for him the next two weeks off."

Sweeter Than Wine 177

"He did?" she said, incredulous.

He nodded. "Saw the man in the lobby with his bags. He told me Mr. Stuart had suddenly given him the time off. Said he would be gone for a while and wouldn't need him."

There must be some mistake. He couldn't be gone.

The man was staring at her quite curiously, and she realized that her doubts must be mirrored on her face. Smiling quickly, she thanked him for his information and turned back toward the parking lot.

Before she had taken two steps, a figure emerged from the shadows and a hand grasped her arm.

"You thought I'd left you again, didn't you, Diana?" His smile was sardonic. "You have as much to learn about not believing everything you hear, or even everything you see, as I do."

"James!" She was so glad to see him that she laughed out loud.

"I saw you going up to the manager's door, and as I caught up with you, I heard him giving you that story about my leaving. I decided to see if you would swallow the bait, just as I swallowed the bait your father set out for me. And you did, didn't you?"

"Oh, James," she said anxiously, reaching for him with both hands. "I've learned something about that tonight. We've got to talk."

He wrapped her in his strong arms and held her close. "My sentiments exactly," he growled into her hair. "Come on. We'll take the elevator up."

She sat on his long sectional couch and gazed about his apartment while he poured them each a glass of white wine from a chilled bottle. The couch was covered in a raw silk fabric of steel gray and ivory, while the floor was carpeted in a heavy wool shag that gleamed like white snow. Glass-and-chrome tables and chairs helped maintain the modern tone, and the pictures on the gray walls were huge abstracts painted in red, black, and silver.

"It's a good thing you don't have children," Diana commented, sliding her foot along the white carpeting. "Those little sticky fingers and muddy feet would turn this place into basic dirt brown in no time."

James's eyes were strangely hooded. "You don't think I would happily give this up to have a few little monsters of my own?" he asked her quietly.

She avoided his eyes, preferring to ignore his question, and he asked as he came from the other side of the room, "Don't you like my apartment?"

"Very impressive," she hedged, hiding a smile as he sat down beside her. "Did you hire a decorator to give you this sterile image, or did it really come right out of your own soul?"

He grinned into her mischievous face. "Not quite your style, is it?" he said dryly. "Think of it as indicative of my ascetic period. The years before I got you back."

She put her wine glass down very carefully and turned to put her arms loosely around his neck. "Does that mean I'm going to influence your taste?" she asked with interest.

"Of course," he murmured, planting tiny kisses along the neckline of her blouse. "You already did that years ago. You know you spoiled me for anyone else."

She loved the feel of his large hands sliding down her back, then up again to hold her shoulders, and she stretched beneath his touch.

"Oh, James," she breathed. "You'll have to stop that. We must talk."

"Talk away." His voice was muffled in the hollow of her shoulder as he peeled away her blouse to get at her skin. "I promise I'll listen."

"But it's about that last day, that summer. Really,

Sweeter Than Wine   179

James. I think we ought to get it straightened out."

He was pushing her slowly, inexorably back against the cushions of the couch, and she was losing the will to struggle against him.

"Go ahead and straighten," he murmured. "I can talk and make love at the same time."

She giggled as his kisses hit a ticklish spot beneath her ear, but she let him slide her along the couch until she was lying back and he was propped above her, kissing every bit of bare skin he could find.

"But I can't," she complained, and then his mouth was covering hers and the protests were forgotten. Sweet and slow, his lips caressed hers, touching them over and over until her tongue flickered out to welcome him in, and he entered, tasting her love. She felt the warmth again, the deep, energy-sapping languor that made her blood hum in her veins and her spirit soar.

He'd unbuttoned her blouse while she was paying no attention, and when his mouth left hers to make the journey down her neck, down across the hollow of her throat to find its way between her breasts, she was surprised at how easily he removed her clothing.

"You're not talking," she whispered, and when he stopped what he was doing in answer, she opened her eyes and looked right into his. "We must talk," she repeated earnestly.

"There's not a whole lot to say," he mused, leaning against her. He seemed to have finally decided they would have it out, but he wouldn't give up totally on what he really wanted, and his hand curled around her breast, cupping it lovingly. "Except maybe to curse your father. And to curse me for my stupid gullibility."

She nodded. "And me for not having the perception to see that there was something very fishy going on."

He smiled down at her, his blue eyes crystal clear. "It wasn't your fault," he chided gently. "How could you know what was happening behind the scenes?"

She bit her lower lip. "I talked to Millie tonight. She told me what my father did that summer. That he went to persuade you to leave." She reached up a hand and tenderly pushed back a lock of sandy hair that had fallen over his forehead. "What did he say, James? Did he tell you I was in love with Lawrence?"

James shook his head. "No. That wasn't exactly it. With a magnificent piece of luck, he actually hit on a brilliant substitute. He didn't tell me you loved Lawrence better. He told me you *needed* him more."

Diana frowned. "You're going to have to explain that one to me," she said, puzzled.

His face darkened. "All right. I'll give it to you as quickly and succinctly as I can. I was getting ready for your party when your father arrived at my camp. He said you'd sent him. He said you were tired of me, that it had been a schoolgirl lark, and you had come to him, not knowing how to get rid of me any other way. You had asked him to come out and tell me to get lost. That you would be embarrassed if I showed up at your party." He took another deep breath. "That I wasn't good enough for you, and you knew that. The party was going to be a celebration of your engagement to Lawrence Farlow."

"My father said that?" Diana couldn't understand it. She had never thought of her father as a cruel man. "And you believed him?"

"No. Actually, at first I thought he was just a protective father, and I laughed it off. But he acted very cool, shrugged his shoulders, and tried to pretend he was doing me a favor. He said you had chosen Larry, that you were with him at that very moment in your garden gazebo."

Diana froze. She *had* been with Lawrence at about that time. "Go on," she said softly.

"I was just mad enough, and just doubtful enough, to run over and take a look." His hand was working

Sweeter Than Wine

absently on her breast now, as though he had to do something with his restless hostility. "And sure enough, there you were in Lawrence's arms."

"Yes," she breathed, "but it wasn't what you think! I had just told him that I loved you, and he was kissing me kind of... as goodbye."

James shrugged. "It didn't look like it at the time. Suddenly... suddenly it was my relatives all over again, looking down at me, whispering about my bad blood." He shook his head. "I went kind of crazy. I knew that we had been something special to each other. That couldn't have been faked. And I thought you were willing to give it all up for a suitable match, a marriage to someone rich and well-bred—not an ignorant field worker like you thought I was. I couldn't take it, not again."

"So that's why you showed up the way you did," she whispered. "You wanted to hurt me the way you thought I had hurt you."

"Yes."

She looked at him keenly. "Whatever happened to that girl?" she asked, curiosity overcoming her better judgment.

"Cherry?" He shrugged. "We never made it to Las Vegas. I think the Barbary Coast in San Francisco was the extent of our journey. And the next morning I got in touch with my father and shipped out to learn the business in his Bolivian office. I stayed in South America for five years before I dared come back. Then, when I met Lisa and realized she was your sister..."

"You saw a chance for revenge," she finished for him.

He hesitated. "Sort of," he admitted. "I didn't really have a very clear idea of what I was doing. I only knew that I had to hang on to anything that would get me closer to you."

James leaned down to kiss her mouth. "And now that I have you again," he growled, "don't make the mistake of thinking I will ever let you go."

Diana kissed him back. "You know I didn't send my father to tell you that, don't you?" she murmured, holding back her anger. "You know I never even thought those things."

He nodded slowly. "I realize it now. Once I saw you again, once I'd kissed you, I knew it had to be a lie. But it took a while to really convince myself."

"Oh!" Suddenly the rage came crashing through her. "How could he have done such a thing? How could he have ruined my life and your life that way?" She pulled out from under James and jumped to her feet, her energy renewed by the adrenaline of anger. Nervously she began to prowl about the room.

"If I'd known at the time, if I'd even had the slightest idea!"

She looked down at James sitting calmly on the couch. "Well?" she demanded. "Aren't you mad as hell? He took six years of our lives from us!"

James's smile was benign. "I've worked through that anger over the last few days, ever since I realized what must have happened. I'm through with that."

He rose and came to her, taking her in his arms. "Your father was a worried man, clutching at straws to do what he thought would protect his daughter. It was just his luck, and ours, that one of those straws happened to have a very sharp point, and that point found its home in my twisted childhood." He hugged her tight and kissed the top of her head. "It's over now. We've found each other again. Let it go."

As though he still felt the resistance in her, he took her head in his hands. "A very wise person once said that we get our best revenge by living well." He dropped a quick kiss on her nose. "Let's try getting our revenge by loving well."

His mouth on hers was seductive persuasion, and very

Sweeter Than Wine

soon she found herself succumbing. The heady sense of destiny about to be fulfilled was infinitely sweeter than wine could ever be, and Diana thought she might drown in its delicious tide. She clung to James's strong body with an ardor to match his, and when he drew back just when she needed him most, she gazed up at him, blinking with surprise at the clouded trouble in his gaze.

"I need it all, Diana," he whispered huskily, his eyes searching for something in hers. "You're still holding back."

Suddenly she knew what he wanted from her. Smiling with affection, she reached for him. "I love you, James," she said aloud. "I love you, and only you, forever."

His relief was written on his face. "And you'll marry me?" he insisted.

She nodded happily. "I'll marry you. If you promise to hurry up and start on all those little sticky-fingered children we're going to raise."

He grinned with delight, then pulled her close again. "I'm way ahead of you. I've already promised my mother her first grandchild."

Diana softly kissed the smooth skin of his tanned neck. "Is that where you were tonight?" she murmured.

"Yes." His gentle touch was kindling the fire between them again. "I got Benton out of the way so we could have the apartment to ourselves. Then I went over to tell my mother that I finally had you cornered." His teeth nipped her earlobe, stilling her movement of protest. "And now I'm going to love you like you've never been loved before."

"Forever?" she whispered, slipping with him into the flames.

"Forever," he promised, and sealed it with his love.

WATCH FOR 6 NEW TITLES EVERY MONTH!

Second Chance at Love

- ___ 05703-7 **FLAMENCO NIGHTS #1** Susanna Collins
- ___ 05637-5 **WINTER LOVE SONG #2** Meredith Kingston
- ___ 05624-3 **THE CHADBOURNE LUCK #3** Lucia Curzon
- ___ 05777-0 **OUT OF A DREAM #4** Jennifer Rose
- ___ 05878-5 **GLITTER GIRL #5** Jocelyn Day
- ___ 05863-7 **AN ARTFUL LADY #6** Sabina Clark
- ___ 05694-4 **EMERALD BAY #7** Winter Ames
- ___ 05776-2 **RAPTURE REGAINED #8** Serena Alexander
- ___ 05801-7 **THE CAUTIOUS HEART #9** Philippa Heywood
- ___ 05907-2 **ALOHA YESTERDAY #10** Meredith Kingston
- ___ 05638-3 **MOONFIRE MELODY #11** Lily Bradford
- ___ 06132-8 **MEETING WITH THE PAST #12** Caroline Halter
- ___ 05623-5 **WINDS OF MORNING #13** Laurie Marath
- ___ 05704-5 **HARD TO HANDLE #14** Susanna Collins
- ___ 06067-4 **BELOVED PIRATE #15** Margie Michaels
- ___ 05978-1 **PASSION'S FLIGHT #16** Marilyn Mathieu
- ___ 05847-5 **HEART OF THE GLEN #17** Lily Bradford
- ___ 05977-3 **BIRD OF PARADISE #18** Winter Ames
- ___ 05705-3 **DESTINY'S SPELL #19** Susanna Collins
- ___ 06106-9 **GENTLE TORMENT #20** Johanna Phillips
- ___ 06059-3 **MAYAN ENCHANTMENT #21** Lila Ford
- ___ 06301-0 **LED INTO SUNLIGHT #22** Claire Evans
- ___ 06131-X **CRYSTAL FIRE #23** Valerie Nye
- ___ 06150-6 **PASSION'S GAMES #24** Meredith Kingston
- ___ 06160-3 **GIFT OF ORCHIDS #25** Patti Moore
- ___ 06108-5 **SILKEN CARESSES #26** Samantha Carroll
- ___ 06318-5 **SAPPHIRE ISLAND #27** Diane Crawford
- ___ 06335-5 **APHRODITE'S LEGEND #28** Lynn Fairfax
- ___ 06336-3 **TENDER TRIUMPH #29** Jasmine Craig
- ___ 06280-4 **AMBER-EYED MAN #30** Johanna Phillips
- ___ 06249-9 **SUMMER LACE #31** Jenny Nolan
- ___ 06305-3 **HEARTTHROB #32** Margarett McKean
- ___ 05626-X **AN ADVERSE ALLIANCE #33** Lucia Curzon
- ___ 06162-X **LURED INTO DAWN #34** Catherine Mills

Second Chance at Love

- ___ 06195-6 SHAMROCK SEASON #35 Jennifer Rose
- ___ 06304-5 HOLD FAST TIL MORNING #36 Beth Brookes
- ___ 06282-0 HEARTLAND #37 Lynn Fairfax
- ___ 06408-4 FROM THIS DAY FORWARD #38 Jolene Adams
- ___ 05968-4 THE WIDOW OF BATH #39 Anne Devon
- ___ 06400-9 CACTUS ROSE #40 Zandra Colt
- ___ 06401-7 PRIMITIVE SPLENDOR #41 Katherine Swinford
- ___ 06424-6 GARDEN OF SILVERY DELIGHTS #42 Sharon Francis
- ___ 06521-8 STRANGE POSSESSION #43 Johanna Phillips
- ___ 06326-6 CRESCENDO #44 Melinda Harris
- ___ 05818-1 INTRIGUING LADY #45 Daphne Woodward
- ___ 06547-1 RUNAWAY LOVE #46 Jasmine Craig
- ___ 06423-8 BITTERSWEET REVENGE #47 Kelly Adams
- ___ 06541-2 STARBURST #48 Tess Ewing
- ___ 06540-4 FROM THE TORRID PAST #49 Ann Cristy
- ___ 06544-7 RECKLESS LONGING #50 Daisy Logan
- ___ 05851-3 LOVE'S MASQUERADE #51 Lillian Marsh
- ___ 06148-4 THE STEELE HEART #52 Jocelyn Day
- ___ 06422-X UNTAMED DESIRE #53 Beth Brookes
- ___ 06651-6 VENUS RISING #54 Michelle Roland
- ___ 06595-1 SWEET VICTORY #55 Jena Hunt
- ___ 06575-7 TOO NEAR THE SUN #56 Aimée Duvall

All of the above titles are $1.75 per copy

Available at your local bookstore or return this form to:

SECOND CHANCE AT LOVE   Dept. BW
The Berkley/Jove Publishing Group
200 Madison Avenue, New York, New York 10016

Please enclose 75¢ for postage and handling for one book, 25¢ each add'l book ($1.50 max.). No cash, CODs or stamps. Total amount enclosed: $_____ in check or money order.

NAME _____

ADDRESS _____

CITY _____ STATE/ZIP _____

Allow six weeks for delivery.

SK-41

Second Chance at Love

- ___ 05625-1 **MOURNING BRIDE #57** Lucia Curzon
- ___ 06411-4 **THE GOLDEN TOUCH #58** Robin James
- ___ 06596-X **EMBRACED BY DESTINY #59** Simone Hadary
- ___ 06660-5 **TORN ASUNDER #60** Ann Cristy
- ___ 06573-0 **MIRAGE #61** Margie Michaels
- ___ 06650-8 **ON WINGS OF MAGIC #62** Susanna Collins
- ___ 05816-5 **DOUBLE DECEPTION #63** Amanda Troy
- ___ 06675-3 **APOLLO'S DREAM #64** Claire Evans
- ___ 06676-1 **SMOLDERING EMBERS #65** Marie Charles
- ___ 06677-X **STORMY PASSAGE #66** Laurel Blake
- ___ 06678-8 **HALFWAY THERE #67** Aimée Duvall
- ___ 06679-6 **SURPRISE ENDING #68** Elinor Stanton
- ___ 06680-X **THE ROGUE'S LADY #69** Anne Devon
- ___ 06681-8 **A FLAME TOO FIERCE #70** Jan Mathews
- ___ 06682-6 **SATIN AND STEELE #71** Jaelyn Conlee
- ___ 06683-4 **MIXED DOUBLES #72** Meredith Kingston
- ___ 06684-2 **RETURN ENGAGEMENT #73** Kay Robbins
- ___ 06685-0 **SULTRY NIGHTS #74** Ariel Tierney
- ___ 06686-9 **AN IMPROPER BETROTHMENT #75** Henrietta Houston
- ___ 06687-7 **FORSAKING ALL OTHERS #76** LaVyrle Spencer
- ___ 06688-5 **BEYOND PRIDE #77** Kathleen Ash
- ___ 06689-3 **SWEETER THAN WINE #78** Jena Hunt
- ___ 06690-7 **SAVAGE EDEN #79** Diane Crawford
- ___ 06691-5 **STORMY REUNION #80** Jasmine Craig
- ___ 06692-3 **THE WAYWARD WIDOW #81** Anne Mayfield

All of the above titles are $1.75 per copy

Available at your local bookstore or return this form to:

SECOND CHANCE AT LOVE
The Berkley/Jove Publishing Group
200 Madison Avenue, New York, New York 10016

Please enclose 75¢ for postage and handling for one book, 25¢ each add'l. book ($1.50 max.). No cash, CODs or stamps. Total amount enclosed: $ _____ in check or money order.

NAME _____

ADDRESS _____

CITY _____ STATE/ZIP _____

Allow six weeks for delivery.

SK-41

WHAT READERS SAY ABOUT SECOND CHANCE AT LOVE

"SECOND CHANCE AT LOVE is fantastic."
—*J. L., Greenville, South Carolina**

"SECOND CHANCE AT LOVE has all the romance of the big novels."
—*L. W., Oak Grove, Missouri**

"You deserve a standing ovation!"
—*S. C., Birch Run, Michigan**

"Thank you for putting out this type of story. Love and passion have no time limits. I look forward to more of these good books."
—*E. G., Huntsville, Alabama**

"Thank you for your excellent series of books. Our book stores receive their monthly selections between the second and third week of every month. Please believe me when I say they have a frantic female calling them every day until they get your books in."
—*C. Y., Sacramento, California**

"I have become addicted to the SECOND CHANCE AT LOVE books...You can be very proud of these books....I look forward to them each month."
—*D. A., Floral City, Florida**

"I have enjoyed every one of your SECOND CHANCE AT LOVE books. Reading them is like eating potato chips, once you start you just can't stop."
—*L. S., Kenosha, Wisconsin**

"I consider your SECOND CHANCE AT LOVE books the best on the market."
—*D. S., Redmond, Washington**

*Names and addresses available upon request